The Miner's Daughter

Gretchen Moran Laskas

Simon & Schuster Books for Young Readers

New York London Toronto Sydney

SIMON & SCHUSTER BOOKS FOR YOUNG READERS
An imprint of Simon & Schuster Children's Publishing Division
1230 Avenue of the Americas, New York, New York 10020

SIMON & SCHUSTER BOOKS FOR YOUNG READERS
is a trademark of Simon & Schuster, Inc.
Book design by Einav Aviram
The text for this book is set in Adobe Garamond.
Manufactured in the United States of America
2 4 6 8 10 9 7 5 3 1
Library of Congress Cataloging-in-Publication Data
Laskas, Gretchen Moran.
The miner's daughter / Gretchen Moran Laskas.— 1st ed.
p. cm.
Summary: Sixteen-year-old Willa, living in a Depression-era West Virginia mining town, works hard to help her family, experiences love and friendship, and finds an outlet for her writing when her family becomes part of the Arthurdale, West Virginia, community supported by Eleanor Roosevelt.
ISBN-13: 978-1-4169-1262-0 (hardcover)
ISBN-10: 1-4169-1262-2 (hardcover)
1. Depressions—1929—West Virginia—Juvenile fiction. [1. Depressions—1929—West Virginia—Fiction. 2. Coal mines and mining—Fiction. 3. Family life—West Virginia—Fiction. 4. West Virginia—History—20th century—Fiction. 5. Arthurdale (W.Va.)—History—20th century—Fiction.] I. Title.
PZ7.L32719Min 2007
[Fic]—dc22
2006000684

FIRST
F
EDITION

For my grandmother Colleen Riggleman Moran,
a true miner's daughter.
And in memory of my grandfather Bruce Moran,
taken too soon by black lung.

Acknowledgments

I personally owe a debt to many people, beginning with two original settlers of Arthurdale, the late Beulah Myers and the late Ellen Eaststep. I'm grateful to the Appalachian Writers Workshop and fellow writer Silas House. This novel became reality due to the efforts of my agent, Mel Berger; my editor, Julia Richardson; and everyone at Simon & Schuster. I would be lost without the help of Laura Ruby and Anne Ursu.

My English teacher, the late Ardith Beets, introduced me to Willa's poetry. School librarian Eleanor Gaudio made sure I found all the right books. My school newspaper editor Stephen Bednar taught me that it isn't only what we say but how we say it that gives words their power. I hope this novel shows that I really was paying attention!

As always, my family, past and present, taught me that

one person can make a difference. My mother and father, Gerald and Emily; what Mom didn't teach me, Dad taught me to find at the library. My sisters, Laura and Gerallyn. My mother-in-law, Elfrieda Laskas. To my husband, Karl, thank you for taking my hand in yours. For my son, Brennan, thank you for taking in stride a mother who sometimes gets so lost in thought that she walks into walls.

And lastly, this novel would never have been written without the sacrifice and efforts of coal miners in West Virginia and elsewhere, along with their families, who find the strength to send them to work every day. Thank you for going down into the darkness so we might have light.

Chapter One

Willa lingered around the water spigot as long as she could, wishing she had somewhere else to go but back home. Normally she would have been ashamed to be seen wearing her old green dress; the top was so tight that she couldn't even lift her arms. Along the bottom a bright band of color showed where the hem had once been, before Mama had let it out as far as it would go. Even so, the limp, faded skirt just covered Willa's bare knees. If they hadn't needed the rinse water in order to finish the last of the chores, Mama never would have allowed Willa to come down the hillside and into town. But today, with most of the men and boys working in the mine, Riley was almost deserted. The women were taking advantage of the bright October day to get a few loads of washing done, and almost everyone waiting for water was dressed as shabbily as she.

She didn't escape notice altogether. Mrs. Hamden came up, peering over her long, thin nose. "Must be wash day up at the Lowell place," she said, her eyes taking in every last threadbare spot of Willa's dress. "You been down here often enough this morning." Her own empty pails clattered in her hand.

"Yes, ma'am," Willa answered. She couldn't stand Mrs. Hamden—even Mama didn't like her. "Her nose is always in your business," Mama would say, moving her head just like a sniffing dog. And somehow, although Mama, tiny as she was, didn't look anything like scrawny Mrs. Hamden, she could change her whole face, almost convincing Willa and her brothers and sister that it wasn't their mother at all, but their neighbor who was now standing in the room with them. Mama could always make them all laugh by imitating the people around them.

"Bet your daddy, he's glad to have both him and your brother working right now," Mrs. Hamden continued. "You can be making good money with two, though not as good as with four." If Mrs. Hamden started bragging about her three sons, there would be no stopping her. Willa almost stepped out of the line—any moment now the sharp words she was thinking would spring forth from her tongue. But leaving itself would be almost as rude, and Mama wouldn't like hearing that about her daughter. Willa sighed. Mama would be sure to hear, too; it was impossible to keep anything a secret in a coal camp as small as Riley Mines.

(And Willa was most anxious right now to keep her mother from hearing anything that might worry her.)

"Yes, ma'am," she said again, as politely as she could, but she allowed herself the pleasure of turning from the woman. She heard Mrs. Hamden sniff.

Someone called Willa's name, and she turned to see her friend Roselia running over to her. "Guess what happened over at the school today," she burst out. Everyone in the line turned to the girl with the hair so black it looked almost blue, her voice so eager it came out in bursts. "Little Milo Smizak took the teacher's colored chalk—the whole boxful—and when the teacher was out at recess, he came back and Milo had drawn this picture of him yelling at the whole class on the blackboard!"

All around them, there were whispered comments. "He's old enough to know better," one woman muttered.

"About what you'd expect, from a bit of foreign trash," Mrs. Hamden said, not bothering to lower her voice.

Willa froze, waiting to see if Roselia would pay her any mind. But her friend didn't even bother to look up, although Willa saw her cheeks get red. The Olivettis had come from Italy years ago, yet they were still treated as outsiders by many. Willa couldn't stand it; she hated knowing there was nothing she could say aloud that wouldn't get back to Mama. "Reminds me of the time I wrote on my own house," Willa said, trying to sound casual, but she made sure that Mrs. Hamden heard.

"I wish I'd seen it," Roselia said sighing, as though Willa was describing a beautiful dress or a fancy dinner party. "You always were one for scribbling things down any chance you got. But using your house for a tablet!"

"Well, I was barely six years old. About the same age as Milo, I guess." Willa had taken a piece of partly burned coal, as soft and sooty as any pencil, and used it to write her newly learned letters on the front wall of the cabin.

Although it had been ten years since she'd done it, Willa still took a peculiar pride in the neat way the letters had looked: the inky black against the bright whitewash. But the coal company had been furious; their man had come up the hill that same day, demanding that Daddy redo the entire house. With no cash money on hand, the family would have to pay for the whitewash and brushes out of Daddy's future earnings, and that meant they had to go into debt down at the company store. Mama had insisted that Willa help with the painting, and she'd spent three long days working in the sun. Even today, the smell of lime brought back the memory so clearly Willa's arm would ache in sympathy. In the end, Mama had been pleased, because it meant they had the cleanest, whitest cabin on the hillside—at least for a little while. Until the black coal dust settled once again over everything.

Now the coal companies didn't bother with the houses. Nothing in Riley Mines had been painted or whitewashed in over three years. "It's the Depression," the company man told them. That was his answer to everything: from why they didn't bother with the houses, to why there wasn't much work. Weeks went by when the men didn't work at all, although sometimes the little boys were allowed in the mines because the company could pay them less and off the books. Everyone had been surprised and pleased that there'd been work these past few weeks, but Willa's older brother, Ves, insisted it was only because the election was coming up—the coal company was afraid of Roosevelt besting Hoover.

Willa didn't care why the men were working; she was just glad they were. She found it hard to concentrate on elections. What did they matter when Mama was so poorly? She turned back to her friend.

"Who told you about the picture?" Willa couldn't help but wish that she were still a student. She'd loved school, the few years she'd been able to go. But sixteen-year-old girls didn't do such things, especially if you were the oldest girl with a younger brother and sister to help care for. More than anything, Willa loved to read and write; that hadn't changed since she'd made those scrawls on the cabin walls. She was the best reader in the family, not that there was much call for it. The only things to read in the Lowell family were a book of Psalms Mama had won as a child and the few pamphlets and notices the coal company put out.

"You know Theresa," Roselia said. "She comes home every day, filled with news." Eleven-year-old Theresa Olivetti was a lot like her sister—both were great storytellers: life was one endless drama, to hear them tell it. "She said the teacher was going to whip him, but Milo hightailed it out of there."

"Wonder if they'll let him back in," Willa said. The line moved and it was her turn at the spigot. Willa carefully filled her first bucket to the brim. She'd spill some on the walk up, so she liked to make them as full as possible at the start.

Roselia stepped back, as the water gushed out. "You think you can come down to our place this afternoon? Seems like I haven't talked to you in years."

"If Mama will let me," Willa answered. She knew that was unlikely, but she couldn't bring herself to admit it. Willa was too worried about Mama right now to tell even her best friend.

Just then, Mrs. Olivetti called out from her cabin door, "Roselia, come home . . . ," the words rising and rolling like music notes all the way to the women in line.

"Mama thinks I'm Theresa's age," Roselia muttered, but she went home willingly enough, after giving her friend a quick hug. Willa watched her go, seeing how happy and healthy Mrs. Olivetti looked. A lost, lonely feeling crept around Willa.

She didn't hurry, filling her second bucket.

"Must not be much work to be done, if Roselia can gad about, carrying tales," Mrs. Hamden said.

Willa spoke before she thought. "Roselia's the fastest worker I know," she said. "No one scrubs a floor quicker than she does." The Olivetti cabin was one of the cleanest in the camp; Mrs. Olivetti was as particular about hers as Mama was about theirs. Willa couldn't seem to go more than a minute without remembering her mother, who had awakened that morning with hands and feet swollen nearly twice their normal size. She'd hardly been able to move them.

The sniffing sound again. "You wouldn't catch me in one of their cabins," Mrs. Hamden said. "Foreigners is all dirty on the inside, no matter what they look like out. Wouldn't let my girl hang around them; lie down with dogs get up with fleas, as my granny used to say."

Turning back to the spigot, her bucket nearly full, Willa put her left foot behind the pail she'd already filled. As she turned around, the foot seemed to slip, dumping water all over the lower part of Mrs. Hamden's dress and feet.

"You clumsy girl!" the woman shrieked.

"I'm sorry, Mrs. Hamden," Willa said, trying to make her voice match her words. But it was hard; for the first time all day, she felt a beat of laughter. Wait until she told Mama! She might scold, but she'd smile too. Roselia wasn't the only one who could tell a good story. Turning on the spigot full blast, Willa refilled her bucket and headed up the hill.

Mama was sitting on the steps, playing finger games with Kyle. "A rabbit has two long ears," Willa heard her say. "They hop around like this." She moved her hands and the five-year-old boy laughed.

When she saw Willa, Mama turned to her. "Did you know that your brother has never seen a rabbit?" She sounded outraged. "Or even a squirrel? And his mother a farm girl!" Mama's long, silvery hair sparkled in the sun.

Willa thought about it. "I couldn't tell you the last time I saw one," she admitted. She set the water inside the house and joined them on the steps. "Not all that many animals in Riley, other than a few dogs and cats roaming about."

"Not a good place for animals. Plants neither." For years, Mama had tried to put in a garden, but less grew every year in the hard, gritty ground. Willa could remember when there had been a few trees scattered about, left over from when they built the town, but over the years the men had cut them down, using the timber to brace the mine when the company would not. During the boom years, when the coke ovens were going full blast, the air had been so heavy with soot that not even birds flew over then.

"Well, I don't mind telling you," Mama said, standing up and pulling her hair into a loose knot that meant it was time they were all getting back to work, "that if I saw a rabbit today, I'd take off chasing it. Rabbit stew would be a welcome change. Even a groundhog would look pretty good to me, and that's saying something." Laughing, Mama went over to the clothesline and ran her hands over the overalls and shirts to test for dryness.

But Willa didn't feel like laughing at all. Mama's usual brisk walk was now only a lumbering jerk. There was no way she'd be chasing rabbits, even if one were so foolish as to come into the coal camp. Her heavy, pregnant belly showed between the open buttons of her dress, the skin firm and pink.

"Here, Mama," Willa said. "Let me finish the laundry. You go in and have a rest."

For a long moment, Mama looked at Willa. Though her Mama's face frightened her, Willa did not look away. The skin around Mama's eyes was so swollen and tight; Willa had once seen her brother Kyle lovingly stroke his mother's face, the marks of his fingers lingering in the flesh long after he'd turned away.

"You doing all right?" Willa asked. She kept her voice even, when she really wanted to start shrieking or crying. Just last night her ten-year-old sister Seraphina had come home upset, throwing herself into Mama's arms for comfort. But at sixteen, Willa was too old for that, and the hug itself would only make Willa all the more aware of Mama's stretched body and baby waiting to be born; a pregnancy that seemed to grow more dangerous with every passing day.

Mama hesitated. "A rest might do me some good," she said at last, reaching out and tucking a tangle of Willa's hair behind her ear. "Thank you."

As Willa pulled dresses from the line, gathering them against her so they wouldn't drop into the dust, her ear still remembered her mother's touch. Perhaps, she thought, there is always a mark, when another person touches you, an invisible thread connecting you to them. Even when she walked back to the cabin with all the clothes in her arms, so little, it seemed, for a family of six with another on the way, Willa could still feel where her mother's gentle hand had been.

Chapter Two

The weeks leading up to election day were busier than Willa had ever remembered. The men worked round the clock, sometimes doing double shifts after months of being idle. Women walked tentatively around the company store, making choices over shoes and foodstuffs they had denied themselves until they had all but forgotten they were ever desired. Despite the Depression, prices were still high—the coal company could charge whatever it wished and often did. "Not like we able to go anywhere else," Mrs. Olivetti had once pointed out, when someone complained. She was holding some scrip in her hand, which was only good at Riley. All too often the company would print these slips of papers and give them to the workers instead of cash money they could spend anywhere.

Still, the overall feeling in the town was good. Mama was pleased too. "There's talk that they're going to whitewash the cabins," she told them one night at supper. They were eating fried potatoes and onions, with biscuits covered with red-eyed gravy, all food Willa had made without assistance. She was particularly proud of her biscuits—this batch had come out just as light and fluffy as Mama's. Daddy had commented on how good they were, with his first bite.

Though she'd never said anything, Willa had taken over much of the household work. She woke every morning at dawn to fix breakfast for her father and brother and pack their dinner buckets. Then she saw to the tasks of the day—whether laundry, ironing, scrubbing the little cabin, or making sure Kyle and Seraphina were cared for. Just making sure there was enough hot water to wash twelve hands was a huge chore. And then, as the sun was setting and Willa thought she'd never be able to move another step, there was still supper to prepare, and the dishes to wash.

Only the feeling of pride she felt in doing for Mama and the family kept her going. Willa knew that Mama needed her. Instead of putting up a fuss, Mama had simply let Willa do a little more, a little more. But she'd taken to putting her swollen hand on her oldest girl's arm every so often, as though giving Willa what little strength she had.

"They won't whitewash nothing. This working we're all doing, it's nothing more than a trick," Ves insisted. He banged his hand on the table so hard the tin plates jumped. "The minute Roosevelt's elected, they'll shut this place down tighter than a drum."

"You know that for a fact?" Daddy asked. He reached for another biscuit, smiling at Willa.

"I know that they're emptying the mountains as fast as we can dig it out, but the coal's just sitting there, down along the river. They ain't running any more barges than they have the last few years."

"Still might mean things are changing for the better," Mama said. "I can't remember the last time you had work steady like this."

"Four years ago, likely," Ves said angrily. "When they was trying to get Hoover in the first time. And the men are falling for it. Tell them it's an election year and they just stare back at you like a herd of sheep." In the dim light, Ves's dark eyes burned and his thin face looked almost hollow. Willa put some more potatoes on his plate, glad there was some extra to offer.

"I think you and Mr. Roosevelt can rely on people's memories," Daddy said. "We all know what it's been like, these past years."

"Well, I just wish I could get out there and do something about it," Ves muttered.

"I know, son. But right now, let's enjoy the plenty and eat in peace." Daddy glanced over at Mama, who was sitting in the only chair they had—the rest of them stood while they ate. Mama picked up a piece of potato, then put it down again. Ves's eyebrows went up, but he didn't say anything.

Willa knew that she wasn't the only one worried about Mama. Ves's head might be filled with politics—he wished more than anything that he could vote—but her eighteen-year-old brother had, as she had, taken to doing what he could. He kept the coal bin full. Also, he was a good scout for things others missed—like the week before when he'd come home with a fistful of bent, rusty nails that he scoured with sand and straightened with an old hammerhead scavenged a few months before. Then he'd pounded the nails into the thin walls of the cabin, trying to keep it together as the fall winds picked up. Willa often woke in the morning to see two fresh pails of water sitting by the stove. She wasn't surprised that he went out while it was still dark; everyone in Riley knew that water toting was women's work. The other boys would laugh at Ves if they saw him carting pails up the hill.

And just today he'd come back from the mines with two apples in his pocket. He'd cut them leisurely, pretending to be nonchalant, but Willa noticed that Mama received the biggest piece. When he offered a slice to Willa, she shook her head. "Let Mama have it," she said. "I'm not hungry." Which wasn't true at all, especially when she looked at the apples—so sweet that a trickle of juice ran down Ves's hand.

"If Willa don't want it, I sure do," Seraphina said.

"You had plenty," Ves told her, and handed the piece to Mama. She'd thanked him, broken it in two, and shared it with the smaller girl.

As much as she was needed at home, Willa couldn't help but be jealous of her brother. He could waltz in with an apple, and everyone made over him as though he'd handed them the moon, while Willa often felt invisible. Oh, Ves worked hard, sometimes as hard as Daddy, but he was able to help the family without being stuck inside a hot house, away from the hustle of town with all its bits of news and juicy gossip. Willa couldn't quite figure out how she never seemed to see anyone—she hadn't visited with Roselia in days—but she never had a moment to herself, surrounded as she was with endless, boring housework that came undone the moment you'd finished it. How did Mama stand the monotony of patching Kyle's breeches over and over, or keeping the stove going without letting it flare out of control? This day-in-day-out keeping a family together without more than a few pennies at a time was harder than she'd expected. It wearied her in spirit, although she was certainly strong enough in body.

Willa even missed going for the water, and the chance to hear who might be getting married or having a baby.

Seraphina skipped school as often as she went, and even on the best days wasn't one anyway for bringing home stories. Maybe that was why, when Ves said he was going to take a walk after Mama and the little ones had gone to bed, Willa announced that she was coming too. She knew that women didn't wander about Riley at night, but she felt trapped in the little house; her feelings went so deep that she often imagined herself exploding, taking the walls down with her.

"Please, Daddy?" she wheedled.

"Well," he said, running his hand over his head. "With all this election talk, there might be trouble."

"We'll head up the mountain, instead of down," Ves said. Daddy looked relieved and nodded, but Willa was disappointed. She'd wanted to go into town. Still, she was determined to enjoy every bit of this unexpected freedom—even if it was only a taste—of walking around when she usually would have been going to sleep.

"Where are we going?" she asked her brother, as she followed him past the last row of miners' cabins perched against the hillside. She and Roselia had often walked all the way down the coal camp road to the blacktop, two miles away, but they'd never hiked up and over the mountain.

"Just a place I know," Ves told her. "An old pioneer cabin that's practically fallen down, but it's as good a place to sit and think as any."

"You sit and think a lot?" she asked him, surprised. His whole life seemed one of action and movement to her. It was hard to imagine him being still. She wondered what he thought about.

"Sometimes," he answered. They had left the town behind them, and the Harvest moon shone so brightly that Willa could make out the valley on the other side. "It's so beautiful," she said, stopping to stare out over the trees that lined the next mountain over; the tops of them stretched as delicate and lovely as a piece of lace run about a hem. Here, the earth had been left as it had always been. There was no smoldering slag pile; no houses stacked one on top of the other like ladder rungs. The stream below ran like a silver pencil line.

"You should see it in daylight, especially in early spring. The green is so bright it hurts your eyes. Right now, it's all just black and white."

Willa didn't care. She was used to a world of ashy grays, the brightness bleached from the town as thoroughly as the colors had faded from the clothing on their backs. "To think it's been here, this whole time," she marveled. "No wonder the old settlers built a cabin up here. Would be worth the walk, just to look out over this every morning." They sat down on a large flat rock that had once been the cabin's front step. Only the piled stones around the foundation and a few barren Rose of Sharon bushes remained to show that anyone had ever been here.

"Would be an awfully far hike from the spigot every morning," Ves said, with a chuckle.

She joined in. "You should know." Now that they were alone together, Willa wasn't sure where to begin. As close as she and Ves were in age, they had so often seemed more apart than even she and Seraphina; they'd never sat down and talked like this. "I appreciate it, you know. The water you've been hauling."

"That's nothing," Ves said. "I see how hard you're working. When you turned down that apple today, I wished I could run down to the store and pick you up one all for yourself."

"Thanks," she said, pleased that he'd noticed. Perhaps they weren't so different after all. "Are you as scared as I am?" Even as she spoke, she felt a curious easing; she felt lighter, as though she'd taken off a heavy coat, one that had been drenched in water and weighed her down.

She felt, rather than saw, her brother's body relax, as though he felt the same. "Probably," he said. "You remember how my own mother died?"

Willa caught her breath. "I'd forgotten," she admitted. Ves had been a baby when Daddy and Mama married after his mother had died giving birth to him. "I married Waitman for his baby's eyes," Mama used to tease. "They were the most solemn eyes I'd ever seen and I wanted the challenge of making them laugh." But she hadn't made that joke in an awfully long time.

"Daddy tried to get her to see a doctor, but she won't hear of it," Ves said.

Willa nodded. "I asked her about it, but she acted like she hadn't heard me."

"She heard you," Ves said, yawning, and Willa remembered how early he rose every morning. "But like all of us, she's a brick. I can tell by looking that she's proud of you."

Willa felt her cheeks warm. "She's never said anything."

Ves shrugged. "You know that's not their way. But they mean it, all the same."

"I know," Willa said, thinking of her mother's hand touching her arm. A fierce rush of love ran through her. "I've been doing more, but I'll do better," she vowed. She wasn't sure if she was speaking to Ves or the night sky; Daddy was the son of a preacher, and he sometimes talked about God living out beyond the stars.

"You're doing great, kid," Ves told her. He stood up and stretched. "You about ready to head back?" His voice sounded happier, not bitter as it had been back at the table.

"I guess," she said, giving the valley another look before she turned away. Like her brother, she felt better than she had in weeks. And why? Nothing had really changed; Mama was still poorly and the election day tension was thick in the air. But just seeing the beautiful valley had helped. Knowing it was there, even if she couldn't see it every day, made her heart beat faster.

"He's right," Willa burst out.

"Who is?" Ves asked. They had come over the ridge, and the electric lights of the town formed a thin string of yellow glare below. All along the hills, the houses sprouted like mushrooms, dark and squat.

"I was just thinking about what Daddy always says, when something goes his way—how it 'puts heart in a man.' That's how I feel."

Ves smiled, and Willa could see his white, even teeth. "I'm glad you asked to come with me," he told her. "I live too much in my own head sometimes. Talking to you helped."

Willa stopped so quickly that Ves almost ran into her. "What now?" he asked.

"What you just said. About talking." She started walking again, keeping her voice low as they approached the Lowell cabin. "That's what did it. Words matter. People act like they don't—even Mama and Daddy forget sometimes. But they do. At least they matter to me."

"You're a strange one sometimes," Ves told her, "even if you are my sister." Together they tiptoed up the steps and went inside.

Chapter Three

Willa and Mama were walking back up the hill from Riley when Mama stopped and put her hand to her back. "You all right?" Willa asked, letting go of Kyle's hand to take her mother's arm.

"I think so," Mama said, but she sounded out of breath. "Just a twinge. I'll be glad enough to be home."

"You shouldn't have been out today," Willa scolded. "I don't care what Ves said. One less vote for Roosevelt wouldn't matter none."

Mama's eyebrows shot up. "You brave enough to say that to your brother?" She started walking again, though slower, and Willa knew every move took great effort. Kyle had run on ahead, and now sat on their front step, his bare feet kicking at the wood. He grinned at them. "Besides," Mama spoke between footfalls, "it's good to vote. Not often a woman like me gets to be a part of history itself."

Willa kept fussing. "This air can't be good for you." The day was sunny, but cold and windy. "And you're likely over-tired. The way Ves was carrying on this morning at the crack of dawn, you'd think that he was personally respon-sible for making sure it didn't rain."

Mama wobbled, but stayed on her feet. "I don't think it's the wind, giving me trouble," she said in a voice that sounded very far away, as though it had been blown out of her.

For a long minute—a lifetime of minutes, it seemed just then—Willa didn't understand. But when Mama smiled faintly, everything fell into place. "It's your time," Willa said. It was not a question.

"Seems to be," Mama agreed.

"Do you want the doctor?"

Mama shook her head. "No," she said firmly. "After all the babies I've borne, I know well enough what to do."

But Willa didn't—her mother had never told her much of anything about babies and how they were born.

Once inside, she settled Mama on the straw tick, spreading the best quilt over her. "The Granny quilt will make you feel better," she told her mother, running her fingers over the brightly colored pieces embroidered with the signs of the zodiac. It was Mama's prized possession, and just seeing it on the bed made Willa feel more in con-trol. "You need anything? Some coffee maybe?"

"I'm fine," Mama said. Her eyes were closed. "You'd better take Kyle down to the MacGregors'. They know to expect him and Seraphina too, when you see her." Willa wondered where her sister might be; school was closed on election day, and Sera had taken off first thing.

"What do we do now?" she asked.

"We wait," Mama said.

All that afternoon, Willa waited. Not that she was idle; between running back and forth to the water spigot, she did a load of laundry and hung it up to dry. There wasn't much in the way of clothes and diapers for the new baby, but Willa ironed what they had, making them as fresh and crisp as she could. Once, when a soft moan rose from the other room, she stopped and listened. Not until Willa smelled something burning did she turn back to her work. A small scorch mark made a rust-red stain on the night-dress, but Willa was too relieved that Mama was quiet again to care much.

Seraphina came home about dinnertime, banging the door on her way in. "Town's gone wild. You should have heard all the cussing," she announced with obvious relish before Willa could shush her. Mama frowned on swearing, and this was the last thing in the world Willa needed for her to overhear.

"Mama's resting," she said, not sure how much to tell her

sister. "Why don't you have a bite of supper and then head down to the MacGregor house? They're waiting for you."

"Is it the baby?" Sera asked. Willa nodded. "Well, I'll stay here then. Help take care of Mama." As if to prove the point, she dropped down in the chair, her thin arms and legs sprawled over it like a spider in a web.

"We don't need any help," Willa told her sharply. "What we need is you out of the way."

"Well, I ain't going," Sera snapped back.

Willa sighed. The town wasn't the only thing going "wild" around here, what with Mama so ill and everyone too busy to pay Seraphina much attention. Her dress was filthy, as though she'd been playing in mud. Maybe she had; how would Willa know? She resolved to make it up to her younger sister, but just not right this minute. "What would it take to make you go?" she asked, looking around the kitchen, wishing there was even a scrap of scrip she could give her sister for a piece of penny candy. But there wasn't much—just the cornbread Willa had made for dinner and a few cold baked potatoes she'd planned for the meal.

Then she remembered the coffeepot.

"If you go, I'll let you have a cup of coffee," she offered.

Seraphina straightened up. "A whole cup?" she asked.

"A whole cup," Willa agreed. She went over to the stove and poured, trying to keep her hand steady. Mama would scold when she found out, Willa knew. Although plenty of

Riley children drank coffee from age six or even younger, Mama had insisted that Willa and Ves wait until they were twelve. Sera was just ten, and there wasn't as much as a drop of cream or a spoonful of sugar to cut the bitterness. "Drink it up and go."

At the first gulp, Seraphina made a face and looked a little green around the mouth. Slowly, watching her older sister, she drank every drop. Then she stood up and walked out to the porch. Willa couldn't help smiling when she heard Seraphina retching under the porch. But her sister came back in with her chin held high, took a quick peek at Mama, and then headed out without a word.

Willa went back to waiting.

Come evening, Mama let out a scream. Willa rushed in to her, but Mama didn't stop screaming, even when she grabbed both the girl's hands so hard that Willa herself cried out. "You need the doctor?" Willa asked, wondering what to do. Did women always scream like this?

"I don't remember it hurting this bad," Mama murmured when the pain had passed. Willa didn't know if she was telling her to get the doctor or not, but when Mama started another high-pitched wail, Willa knew she had to do something.

"You hold on," she told Mama, although her words were lost in the noise. "I'm going to fetch the doctor."

Willa stumbled at first, as though she too were burdened with a heavy body, but she soon raced down the hill. The polls had closed now, though the town was still crowded with people, mostly men, some of them drinking as they stood against the walls of the company store. A few guards carried guns; she felt them watching her.

Willa dashed down the main street, behind the store and up the small hill where the doctor's house stood. It was bigger than any in the town, except for the coal operators' places that stretched along the road toward the blacktop. Through the large picture window, Willa could see the doctor and his wife sitting down to supper. Tall white candles burned, making the silver cutlery and white china sparkle. Worried as she was, Willa could only stare at the beauty of the table. She stood there, out of breath, her hands pressed up against the glass, looking first at the roast chicken and stuffing, and then at the short, lacy dress the doctor's wife wore. Pearls hung around her white throat.

"Hey, what's the meaning of this?"

A big hand grabbed her shoulder and pulled her from the window. In the glare of the electric light, Willa couldn't make out the man's face—only a dark oval where the eyes, nose, and mouth should be. The man wore a company guard uniform and stank of cigar smoke and whiskey. "Get your filthy hands off that window." He shoved Willa hard, almost pushing her down the porch steps.

"But my mama . . ." Willa gasped. She grabbed the porch railing to catch herself. "I gotta get the doctor . . ."

"Your mama nothing." He loomed over her, so close that she could feel his reeking breath burn her face. "I know what your sort is doing here, pestering the doctor at this hour. Think he'll just hand you something and make the baby go away?" He stared at her unblinking; Willa felt he could see right through her clothes. His hand fell on her shoulder and he squeezed.

"What is going on out here?" A woman wearing a dark dress and an apron came out of the doctor's house. Willa knew this was not the doctor's wife; this woman wasn't wearing any pearls.

"Caught this little scum trying to break into the house," the man said.

"That ain't true!" Willa yelled. "I'm looking for the doctor."

The woman in the doorway stared down at Willa. "Now what business can you be having with the doctor?" the woman asked. She sounded as suspicious as the guard.

"It's my mama," Willa told her. "She's having a baby and she's screaming and carrying on. I don't know what to do." The hand on her shoulder pulled, and Willa heard the fabric tear. Her bare shoulder gleamed in the light.

"Women do scream, sometimes," the woman said. "Who's your daddy?"

"Waitman," Willa said. Maybe it would be all right after all. She took a deep breath. "Waitman Lowell. We live almost at the top of the hill . . ."

"I'll send the doctor up when he gets in," the woman interrupted. "Now, you get on home."

"But he is in!" Willa cried. "I saw him!"

"Get on home now," the woman repeated.

"Don't you worry, ma'am." The guard laughed; the ugliest sound Willa had ever heard. "I know just what to do with this one." His hand moved over the exposed skin where the sleeve had torn; his fingers crept along her collar bone and down her arm.

Willa had never been so frightened. She yanked herself free, feeling the entire sleeve shred, and began to run. She ran away from the bright lights, hoping to hide in the darkest space she could find. She kept running until she was out of breath and was sure the guard was gone.

Although she'd lived most of her life at Riley, Willa didn't recognize a single house along this rutted, twisting road; she was almost to the mouth of the mine itself, and she could see the gaping black doorway where the train tracks vanished. Most of the windows were shuttered, but there was one with a grease lamp burning. Willa pushed closer, trying to peer in. She could smell greens cooked in bacon fat and her stomach rumbled.

"Cans I help you?" a voice said behind her.

Willa opened her mouth to scream, but realized this couldn't be the guard. "I ain't gonna hurt you. You lost, child?" A young woman, her face as dark as Daddy's after a long day in the mine, emerged from the shadows. In the light from the doorway, Willa could see she wore a pretty red dress. "What you called, honey?"

"I'm Willa." This unexpected kindness was too much to bear after the long scare, first at home, then at the doctor's. She burst into tears. "I was trying to get the doctor. It's my mama. She's up there on the mountain having a baby and screaming something awful. I just know something's wrong . . ."

The woman put her arms around Willa. "It's all right, honey."

"I was all alone with her," Willa said. "I don't know what I'm gonna do."

"You cans come with me," the woman in the red dress said, taking her hand. "I knows a good granny who takes cares of women like your mama."

Willa followed the woman down the winding street, hardly more than a path. They stopped outside a tiny house and the woman knocked. "Who's there?" someone asked, opening the door a crack.

"It's Tori," the dark woman answered. "I gots someone who's birthing."

"I'll get my bag." After a moment, the door opened

wide and a woman no taller than Willa came out. If she was surprised that Willa was white skinned, she made no sign. "You come about your mama?" she asked.

"Yes, ma'am," Willa managed to say. She'd never seen anyone so old, so dark.

When Tori started to follow, the old woman reached out and touched her sleeve. "Best stay," she said. "You know they're prowling, looking for trouble."

Willa nodded. "The guard was chasing me, when I tried to get the doctor."

Tori shifted back from one foot to the other. "I'll be all right," the old woman told the young one. Then she turned to Willa. "You come with Granny Maylie now." Silently they walked back into town, skirting around the mining buildings with their bright electric lights before climbing the hill on a side path.

"How long's she been birthing?" Granny asked when they reached the top. She wasn't even out of breath.

"Since about noontime," Willa answered as they approached the house. Once inside, Willa could hear her mama tossing around and moaning. She wondered if Mama had been screaming while they were gone.

Granny went to her and put a hand on Mama's stomach. After a moment, she asked, "Can you build a fire, girl?"

"Yes," Willa told her, glad to be told to create warmth. Her teeth were chattering, although she didn't feel cold.

"Build me a good one and put some water on." Granny turned back to Mama. "You best take this with you," she said, handing Willa the fancy quilt. "It's might pretty work for a birthing room. Take it and rest yourself while you can." Willa quickly built the fire and put on the last of the water she'd carted that afternoon. Then she wrapped the quilt around her and went outside to wait for Daddy and Ves.

Her brother arrived first, and Willa was glad to see he had a bucket of water. "You hear anything? About the election? Over on Scott's Run they handed out whiskey to people who pledged to vote for Hoover . . ."

Willa cut him off. Who cared about some election just now? "The baby's coming," she told him, the story pouring out of her: the long wait, the screaming, the guard. He made a sound then, a low growl deep in his throat, but Willa rushed on. When she mentioned Tori and Granny Maylie a funny look passed over his face. Without saying anything, her brother went inside and she could hear him washing up.

"What do you think Daddy's gonna say?" Ves asked when he came back out. He jerked when he moved, as though he were too nervous to be still. He glanced into the house.

"Nothing," Willa said shortly. "If he wants to go find someone else, then he can. Mama's not screamed once since Granny Maylie came."

"You're probably right," Ves said. He looked down the

ridge in the direction of the black miners' section of the town. "But don't it make you feel kind of funny? Knowing one of them's in there?"

"I feel a lot less funny than I did when it was only me," Willa told him. She pulled the blanket tighter.

"Well, Daddy'll be here any minute, now that the shift's ended," Ves said. They watched the circles of light from the miners' caps bobbing up the hill like fireflies. One by one the lights separated and went out; soon Willa could see Daddy's lamp.

"What are you two doing out here?" he asked. Again she told her story: Mama screaming, the doctor, the guard, Tori, and Granny Maylie.

Inside the house, Daddy dimmed his light. He poured water over his head and hands, his hair dripping wet, not pausing even to change his sooty clothes before opening the door to the room where Mama lay on her straw mattress. Granny Maylie sat next to her, holding her hand.

"How is she?" Daddy asked in a soft voice.

"The baby's gone and turned itself around," Granny Maylie said. "She breeched before?"

"I think Willa here was breech," Daddy answered. "Gave her a hard time."

Mama began to toss and turn; Granny kept moving her hands over Mama's uncovered belly. Ves looked away. "I'm trying to get the baby to go right side up," she said, kneading the firm flesh as Mama's face wrinkled with pain. "Might be awhile."

"Do what you can," Daddy told her. "I'm much obliged." He pushed Willa and Ves from the room. "You two go on out to the porch. I'll be out shortly."

Wrapped under the quilt, Willa listened to the rain that began to fall. After a few minutes, the pounding on the roof was so loud that it drowned out all other sounds around them. Ves should be happy, she thought to herself sleepily. At least it had held off until the election was over. Tomorrow, she'd head up the mountain to the old pioneer cabin and see the other valley washed clean. Mama would be better by then. Over the next few days, women from all over Riley would come bringing what little food they could spare, wanting to see the baby. Maybe Mrs. Olivetti would make some of her homemade noodles with the tomato sauce that Willa liked so much.

"Are you mad, Daddy?" Willa asked. He had come out and sat between them, and they both leaned against him as if they were his youngest ones, not his eldest.

"Mad? At who?"

"I tried to get the doctor," she said. "I did everything I could."

Daddy squeezed her, making her feel warmer and safer than ever. The rain continued to pour. "I'm right proud of you," he said.

"But I ran away," Willa told him. She could still feel the guard's hand on her shoulder, pushing her down the doctor's steps, but mostly she felt the strength of Daddy's arm around her.

"You should have run. That was the right thing to do."

"He tore my dress," Willa mumbled into his shoulder. "It's ruined, I think." He smelled like the mine; a rock dust so strong she could taste it on her tongue.

"Maybe with all this work we've had, we can see about getting you a new one," Daddy told her. "What color would you want?"

On any other day, the idea of a new dress would be exciting, but just now, Willa was too tired. Her last thought was of Tori, in her bright dress. "Red," she answered.

"Red's an awfully grown-up color," Daddy said, a little surprised.

"Red," Willa repeated. Her eyes would not stay open. "You asked."

"So I did. Red it is."

Chapter Four

Granny Maylie said Mama would be in bed a week or so, but after three weeks, she still hadn't risen to do more than make her way to the outhouse around back. She returned to the cabin with a face so pale even the whites of her eyes had more color than the flesh surrounding them. The once magical silver hair was dull and gray now. Sometimes she walked with her hands around her stomach, as though the baby was still inside of her, and not wrapped in clean towels, resting in an old laundry basket next to Mama's bed. The first few times her mother had taken more than a few steps, Willa watched with horror as great clots of blood, the size of chicken's eggs, fell out from under the hem of her nightdress. Their bright red was a shocking spot of color on the ever-dusty floor.

"I'll take care of that," Willa had said, when she saw the distress on Mama's face. "You just get on back to bed."

But even scrubbing the spot with a wire brush wasn't enough. The ugly stains marred the wood like small round footsteps.

Every few days, Granny Maylie came to check on her, bringing herbs and tonics in her black bag. Every few days she came out from Mama's room, her dark face angry and fierce. "Fine time for the doctor to be going by-your-leave," she muttered, shaking her head. But she kept coming, and the family was grateful that there was someone remaining in Riley Mines skilled enough to care for Mama. Willa didn't even begrudge the few pieces of scrip Daddy handed her, or the bag of potatoes; there was no putting a price on all the help Granny had given.

The doctor wasn't the only one in town who was gone. The coal operators, the teachers, the storekeepers—everyone who had any other place to go had packed up and left. Not a week after the election, Ves called to Willa to come out onto the front steps. From there they could see a cloud of dust rising up along the dirt road that led into the village.

"What do you suppose it is?" Willa asked.

"I don't know," Ves said. But they both knew it wasn't anything good. "I'm headed down to see. You coming with me?"

Willa nodded. "I'll bring Seraphina too; will make the house quieter. But I'll tell Mama we're just going for water. I don't want her worried."

As the three of them walked down the hill, they saw the trucks pulling up to the coal company buildings. Riding in the back, perched on top of stacks of newly cut lumber, were men who looked as limp and weary as any Willa knew. But these weren't Riley men. They jumped off the truck with their heads bent down, not meeting anyone's eyes.

"Willa!" Roselia called out. She and her sister Theresa came over and joined the Lowells, who were standing across the street from the company store. "Do you know what's going on?"

"No," Willa said. "You hear anything?"

"Nothing," Roselia answered. If her friend didn't know, Willa knew that no one did.

More and more miners and their families gathered about, but there was no chatter, no calling back and forth. Working in groups of three or four, the hired men began to board up the entrances to the mines, as well as the school, the church, and even the old bowling alley where no one had rolled a ball in nearly three years since the company closed and locked it.

"They could have at least paid us a few pennies to board things up," Ves grumbled, "instead of hiring out. Company doesn't trust us even to make good on that." The armed guards from election day were back; they stood on the corners and peered into the crowd. The sun glinted off the great screws the workmen used to secure the plywood over the windows of the doctor's house and the store.

"Would you want to do this?" Willa practically spat out the words, she was so furious. "Any money would be blood money, as far as I'm concerned. I'd just as soon not be the one who goes home and tells Mama and Daddy that I had any part in it." The pounding of so many hammers seemed to sink down into the ground and drum its way through the soles of her feet.

Another car pulled up, a big black one with chrome as shiny as mirrors. Willa saw a man get out, a man dressed in a blue suit and shirt so white and crisp Willa wondered that she didn't hear him rustling when he walked. She could see the tiny red feather in the crown of his hat; his shoes were whole and new. He didn't look at the miners—not those working for him or those standing around and watching.

But he could shout well enough, and every last person strained to make out what he was saying. Two of the guards pulled a sign out of the car, and when they unfurled it a collective gasp went up from the town, as though together they strained to catch their breath. Even those who did not know how to read understood the word "closed."

"You said it would happen, Ves," Willa said, staring at the sign. "You said after the election they'd close us down."

"What's gonna happen, Willa?" Seraphina asked. She had taken her sister's hand. "What will happen to us?"

"I gotta get out of here," Ves said. He'd clenched his hands into fists, and Willa could see them shaking. "I'm going up the mountain. If you want to come with me, come, 'less you'd rather stay here and watch them destroy what's left of our town."

As her brother spoke, Willa could feel Seraphina getting more and more upset. She put her arm around her sister and tried to put reassurance into her voice that she certainly did not feel. "Sera and I'd better get back. Mama will be wondering how long it takes three people to draw a pail of water."

They left Roselia and Theresa standing there and headed back up the hillside. No one felt like talking, and Seraphina clung to Willa as though she were only Kyle's age instead of the half-grown girl of ten who had only a few weeks ago been drinking coffee in the Lowell kitchen. "What are we gonna do?" she kept repeating over and over, until the phrase grated on Willa's last nerve.

"I don't know yet," Willa snapped at her. "Stop pestering." But she didn't let go of the girl's hand, even when they reached home. Though near the top, the Lowell cabin wasn't high enough to get away from the sound of banging hammers down below. Willa wished they'd stop just long enough to give her a moment to think.

Willa stood there on the steps, straightening her back and trying to put a smile on her face when all she wanted to do was start running, soaring past Ves and everyone else she'd ever known. She'd go beyond the pioneer cabin, down the other side of the mountain and over the creek; she'd keep running until she found a world where the word "Depression" had never been.

Instead, she stood tall. She must be brave for Mama, and Seraphina and Kyle too. "Let's go see how the new baby's doing," Willa called to her sister. As jauntily as she could, she swung the pail in her hand, only to realize that it was dry and empty. With all the noise and confusion going on, she'd forgotten to fill it.

After the mines closed, the rest of the winter became one long and endless blur. Cold set in, and the wind roared down the mountain, over the cabins, seeping through every crack in the walls and up through the floorboards. Ves and Daddy spent several days mixing the gritty dirt with water, patching the grooves between the boards, giving the entire house a frightful look, as though overnight it had been cursed with an outbreak of giant warts.

Inside was not much prettier. Roselia's father, who had worked as a janitor before the school closed, slipped through a small forgotten window he knew had a broken lock and brought out a great pile of newspapers that had been left behind. The two girls spent many hours in each other's homes, crumpling the papers and stuffing the balls into mattress tickings, making the beds a little softer and warmer, even if they crinkled when anyone moved. They sewed the papers between their thin blankets to create extra layers.

Willa held the funny pages back for Kyle and Seraphina to enjoy, and when they had all memorized the lines she tried to make new jokes to suit the yellowing drawings. But even with her best efforts, Willa's stories were not Mama's stories and everybody knew it. Nearly every day, Willa had to taste the bitterness of a life filled with things undone no matter how hard she vowed to do better.

The new baby, who had once been so exciting, began to pall. With hair as red as a shiny new penny, he would bring the family luck, Daddy said, but Willa sometimes thought secretly to herself that since the baby's birth the family had never been as unlucky as it was now. Still, it was something safe to talk about: Ves often teased Mama that folks were going to think she'd gone down to the creek and had him there, his hair the same shade as the orange water. "I don't know where the red hair comes from," Mama said, smiling, looking for the first time in weeks a little like her old self. "Maybe I ate too many carrots before he was born."

But most days Willa thought the baby more trouble than he was worth. Mama's milk was weak, and the baby cried and cried; hours went by when he barely paused long enough to take a breath.

"Why'd you go and have all us kids?" she asked her mother one afternoon. It had been a particularly trying one: Kyle had fallen down and wanted his mother to kiss his bruised knees. Willa's kisses wouldn't do. Seraphina, always clumsy, had fallen against the window, cracking the glass in a long thin streak. Willa had never felt more useless, and something must have shown on her face because Ves stood up and hustled the little ones out of the cabin. She didn't ask where he was going; at that moment she did not care.

As soon as they had gone, Willa went over to her mother's bedside and stared at her mother and Rusty, who were sleeping in a warm nest of newspapers and the Granny quilt. Willa longed to crawl in next to them. After a few moments, Mama's eyes fluttered open and she smiled at her oldest daughter.

"Everything all right?" she whispered.

Willa knew she should say yes, that things were fine. But just thinking the words seemed to choke her. "Kids are nothing but a bunch of work," Willa burst out. "I ain't ever having any."

"Shhh," Mama soothed, and gestured for Willa to

stretch out beside her. To Willa's surprise, being this close to her mother was as comforting as it had been as a child, but was different now that she was sixteen. In a way, it wasn't unlike being next to Roselia, knowing that the night was ripe for the telling of secrets and dreams the way two girlfriends do. No matter how bleak the world had been only moments before, the coziness between mother and daughter thrilled Willa.

"I mean it," Willa said, though the fierceness was gone from her voice. "Young ones are nothing but a pain."

"You'll change your mind someday," Mama said. Willa could feel Mama's breath stir her hair. "I'd have ten more babies if I had the chance. Just watching each of you grow in your own way is like getting a gift that never goes away."

"I'm not like you," Willa whispered. "Seems like I can't turn around but I've done something else wrong."

To her surprise, Mama laughed. "You think I could have kept house the way you are when I was sixteen? Why, the first year I was married, your daddy came home to a cabin where everything was in pieces—especially his wife who was more than likely sitting in a chair bawling and wringing her hands."

"But you make it look so easy," Willa insisted.

"I've had years to learn." Mama propped herself up on one elbow and gazed down at Willa. "Keep in mind I was a farm girl, used to running around outside and making my own way. Those first years in a coal camp were a nightmare to me."

"What happened?" Willa asked.

Instead of answering right away, Mama turned bright red. "Well," she hesitated, "part of getting married means being with another person. You know, loving them." The blush had spread all the way to her ears. "When your daddy and I were together, being so made things seem all right somehow. And knowing that babies came from our love made you all more special too." Mama did not look Willa in the eye, but there was no mistaking the expression of contentment that flitted over her face. "Watching all of you is seeing bits and pieces of all the people Daddy and I have ever loved in new and wonderful ways—like the way you have my mother's musical laugh and Seraphina has my mother's hair. Kyle favors my pap and I think Rusty will take after the Lowells. And Ves . . . Ves at eighteen is your daddy all over again at that age." She shook her head, but Willa knew she was not upset.

Mama brushed the hair from Willa's damp cheek. "Do you know I can still remember the first time you looked up at me and knew I was your mother? You couldn't have been much older than Rusty here, but when I saw that recognition in your eyes I realized that I hadn't left my world behind by marrying your father, but in having you, I'd created my own."

Willa didn't know what to say. Mama could talk end-lessly about almost anything, but had never spoken this personally before. Although the words themselves were few, Willa knew they had expressed much.

Then, as if the words had exhausted her, Mama took a deep breath and lay back down, staring up at the ceiling. Beneath the quilt the world was still and peaceful; Willa didn't realize that she'd fallen asleep until she awoke an hour later in an empty bed, the blanket tucked carefully about her by her mother's gentle hands.

Moments like that one, however, were all too few. The winter dragged on; when Willa wasn't trying to keep her-self and her family warm, she felt haunted by hunger. Night after night she would wake up in the darkness, won-dering that she didn't ring inside, given the emptiness of her belly. Sometimes she could almost feel it coiling inside of her like a great snake, so strong and sure that it seemed almost alive.

No one in Riley Mines had food enough. The company store was only open a few hours, one day a week, mostly to give the men who were stationed as guards a chance to buy what they needed. No miner or his family had more than a few cents that had been earned by leaving the area and putting in a day's work, assuming the men could find any-thing. Daddy and Ves often left before daybreak, walking to the blacktop where there might be someone with money in his pocket looking for a day laborer to do what he couldn't do for himself.

Willa knew that as hard as it was at the Lowells', other families had it worse. Earlier in the summer, when the mines had been slow but still providing, Ves and Daddy had spent their off days working on local farms, helping to bring in the harvest. They'd been paid in produce: corn, beans, squash, and apples. Some of the families had been too large or simply too hungry to do more than eat what came to hand. The Lowells had been able not only to put some of the bounty aside, but also had Mama's precious canning jars from her parents' farm to preserve the provisions safely.

Willa lingered over memories of those hot summer afternoons when she and Mama had canned. Back then, it had seemed that there was so much food, so much heat and light, that thoughts of winter were like waking up and knowing you'd dreamed, but not remembering anything about it except that you had. She tried to recapture what it had felt like, those moments of plenty, as she fixed a batch of thin cornbread—enough for a few bites each. Willa recalled the way the sun had beat down upon their heads, as they dried the corn and then hauled it over their shoulders to the mill to be ground.

No. Winter dreams in summer were hard enough.

Imagining summer in winter only brought out that nightmarish feeling that summer might never come again.

Because Willa knew that this winter was worse than any other had been. Oh, in some ways it was the same. The Lowells had all moved to the one large room of the cabin, to save on heat. But Willa was used to the lack of privacy, the constant rattletrap of noise and movement. She had lived through winters of want before, where families came out of the cabins in springtime looking root-like pale, their bones sharp and poking through their skin. Willa knew that hands that cracked and peeled like tree bark would not always be so rough that she couldn't feel a needle between her fingers. This she had known before, and likely would again.

But this winter, lying awake in the cold, wallowing in hunger, Willa was taken aback by how silent the world around her was. Not the day-to-day noise of the seven of them that filled the days, but the strange stillness of the night. Without the coal roaring down the tipple, without the railcars shunting and banging over the tracks, Riley Mines had become a ghost town of sorts, a ghost town still filled with living people. The silence was so strong it sometimes hurt her ears.

And yet, even that was not the worst. The stillness was better than those nights where Willa would wake and hear Mama crying from her bed across the room. "I'm sorry,

Wait," Mama would say over and over and over. "I'm sorry. I'm sorry. I'm sorry. I just can't."

Daddy would tell her to hush. "Don't cry now, Esther," he whispered to her. "It's gonna be all right. I promise you."

As Willa lay there in the dark, she tried to imagine what Daddy knew that she didn't. As far as Willa could see, it was never going to be better; with the mines closed, how could it be? But just hearing him promise became a lullaby of sorts. The words helped enough that she managed to close her eyes and sleep, until it was time to struggle through another day.

Chapter Five

Willa was scrubbing the front steps, enjoying the warm weather of early April, when she heard Ves's footsteps running for the cabin. "Where's Daddy?" he asked, so out of breath he bent forward as he spoke.

"What's wrong?" she asked, her voice sharp. Spring in 1933 had been late in coming. Willa couldn't help but wonder if even the weather wasn't tired of the Depression. She was tired: tired of working; tired of being hungry; tired of being tired. "You're gonna wear yourself out," Willa told him, wishing she didn't sound so peeved and angry; Daddy would tease, calling her a fishwife if he were here. But they had just got Mama well enough now that she could be up and about again. The last thing Willa could stand would be if something happened to Ves.

Her brother ignored her. "Where's Daddy?" he asked again.

"He was down at the company store, last I saw him," she said. Ves nodded and took off again. Willa called after him, but he paused only long enough to wave and then went on.

"What was that all about?" Mama asked, standing in the doorway. She carried little Rusty on her hip and moved in a slow deliberate way that made Willa wince to watch her.

"He didn't say," Willa answered. She stood up, emptying the bucket of dirty water under the porch. "You need me to do anything else?"

Mama, who had been shading her eyes to peer down into town, dropped her hand and smiled. "I daresay we've done enough for this morning." Willa was relieved. For weeks now, Mama had been on a fit of housekeeping, as though only by cleaning the place from top to bottom every single day they could get all the dirt and grime that had settled there during the winter, when she'd been so poorly. "I know you want to know what Ves is all worked up about, and to tell you the truth, I wouldn't mind knowing myself."

Willa shoved the bucket so hard it fell over with a clang. "As soon as I know, I'll come back and tell you everything!" she called out to her mother as she raced down the hillside. She barely paused, taking pleasure in the very movement of her feet, not stopping even as people greeted her. "Hello, Mrs. Foley," she said, breathlessly rushing past. Mrs. Hamden called out, but Willa gave her only the briefest of hellos; she would sniff, insulted, no matter what Willa did.

As on most afternoons, the men had gathered on the steps of the shuttered company store. The big CLOSED sign that had seemed so shocking and stark when it had been unveiled last November hung tattered now. Willa wondered where the coal dust came from when the mines were closed, for the sign, like everything else in Riley, was streaked gray with it.

Ves stood with Daddy and some other men, talking up a blue streak. Daddy's battered hat was off and he ran his hand over the back of his neck, which meant he was thinking about something.

"But we'd have to leave tomorrow," Willa heard Ves say. "When the truck comes."

"Doesn't give us much time to think it over, now, does it?" Daddy said. He looked up and saw Willa and nodded to her. She went over and stood by him, the only girl in the crowd, wondering what Ves had meant by leaving tomorrow. Just where was there to go?

"I don't think there's anything to think over," Ves said. If he noticed his sister, he didn't pay her any mind. "Ain't like we got much choice."

"Man's always got a choice, son," Daddy said. A few of the men around him nodded.

Ves threw up his arms. "I can't believe it!" he shouted. "We got a real chance here, and no one but me . . ."

Daddy reached out and put his hand on Ves's arm. "No one's saying no. But you sprung this on us awful sudden-like."

"Well, I can go, can't I, Daddy?" Ves asked.

Willa couldn't stand it another minute. "Go where?" she asked.

"Hawk's Nest," Ves told her, as if that would explain everything.

"Hawk's Nest?" she asked. The name meant nothing to her. "Is that another coal camp?"

Ves started to answer, but Daddy shook his head. "Your brother's been telling us about a big industrial project downstate. Seems some company is drilling a tunnel through a mountain and needs men to work."

"They're going to change the direction of a whole river," Ves said; he'd always been excited by big ideas, and this one sounded huge.

"Is this one of Mr. Roosevelt's plans?" Willa asked. She hadn't seen her brother so eager since election day. Heaven knows they'd all been waiting long enough for the new president to do something to change things. As far as Willa was concerned, all that had happened since November was the mine closing down for good.

"I don't know, and I don't think Ves here does either,"

Daddy said. Willa tried to read her father's face; clearly he was wrestling with something deep inside. Daddy wasn't one to put his feelings on display, but just now he couldn't seem to keep control; his face kept changing, the lines curving one way and then the next. "None of us," he said, looking at his son, "knows exactly what this Hawk's Nest is." When Willa heard the shudder of fear, she understood at last what he was trying to hide. All winter, she too had been fighting against the coward inside she knew herself to be.

Daddy put his hat back on his head and took a deep breath. "But what we do know is that the mine isn't gonna reopen this spring." He spoke slowly and, when he paused, he swallowed hard. "And I don't know about you, but it makes a body weary, watching his family going hungry day after day. If my boy tells me there's work downstate and there's a truck headed that way, well." He gently tapped his son on the shoulder with his fist. "I'm only thirty-eight years old. Seems like I ought to be eager enough for one more chance."

Ves let out a whoop so loud Willa could hear it echo off the buildings. The men gathered about were smiling; there was no mistaking the air of hopefulness that raised their chins and steadied their hands. Daddy was laughing, talking about what he was going to do with all the money he made. No one noticed when Willa started walking away.

She tried to think just what she should say to Mama, and how she felt about moving. Mama would have a dozen questions, Willa figured. She'd want to know about the houses, and how far away this Hawk's Nest was. What would the pay be like, and how dangerous was it, to drill through a mountain and turn a river all around? Or maybe she wouldn't care at all. Maybe it was only Willa who was curious about these things. Mama might not feel she had any right to ask, given how hard times were for them. For the first time, Willa realized fully just how desperate everyone around her was. They were desperate to do something, anything, as if by moving about they could convince themselves that they hadn't given in to the very desperation that was driving them so.

"Here I spent all morning on those stupid steps," Willa muttered. "Now we're going to go and leave them before they can even get good and dirty again." Instead of heading for home as she'd promised Mama, Willa stopped off at Roselia's house. Maybe talking things over with a friend would help her know just how she was supposed to feel. She'd not even time to knock on the door before Roselia had opened it and pulled Willa inside.

"Have I got something to tell you!" Roselia said.

Willa nodded. "I know about Hawk's Nest. Daddy says we're going."

"Going?" Roselia asked. "Going where?"

"To Hawk's Nest."

"Where's that?"

Willa was surprised. "Ain't that what you meant, when you said you had something to tell me?

"What's Hawk's Nest?" Roselia demanded. She waved her hands up around her face. "Why are you going there?"

"It's some place downstate," Willa told her. "Daddy said we're leaving tomorrow. I don't know any more about it than that."

Roselia's hands went still and fell to her sides. "You're leaving?"

Willa nodded, her throat closed, every breath painful.

"Oh, Willa," Roselia whispered.

"Maybe you'll be going too?" Willa asked. But she hadn't seen Mr. Olivetti down on the steps, talking with the men and Daddy. Ves had mentioned a truck, but how large could any truck be? Even with as little as any family had, one truck wouldn't be able to take very much or very many.

"No one's said anything to me," Roselia said. She sagged against the door frame.

Willa felt like crying. Why couldn't good news just be good news? Why did it always seem that there was something to be given up? "What did you want to tell me?" she asked. "If it wasn't that?"

"Nothing," Roselia said with a shrug. "It don't matter now. Not if you're going away."

"But what was it?" Willa persisted.

"I was gonna tell you about the missionary lady."

"A missionary lady? Here in Riley?" No one ever came to Riley these days.

Some of the sparkle returned in Roselia's dark eyes. "I think she's a missionary. She looked kind of like a teacher, but she didn't go over to the school or nothing. Went over to the old store—you know the one they closed down a few years ago when they built the new one?"

"What was she doing?"

Roselia straightened. "You want to go see?" she asked, the eagerness back in her step.

They heard the woman before they saw her. She was calling out orders to two men who were unloading a truck filled with boxes. "Be careful with those. I don't want them damaged." Her hands were on her hips, and her back was to the girls.

"What would a missionary need with all those boxes?" Roselia whispered to Willa.

"Whatever's in them, they're heavy enough," Willa said. She didn't know what to think. Strangers in Riley Mines rarely meant anything good.

As quiet as they were trying to be, the woman must have heard them because she spun around, her dark blue skirt flaring out about her. "Hello, there!" she said, waving. "How are you?"

For the first time, Willa saw her friend go absolutely silent. Roselia's mouth was opening and closing, but nothing was coming out.

"Yes, ma'am," Willa said automatically, although she knew that this wasn't an answer to the question of how she was at all. She stared at the woman's short brown hair—Willa had seen pictures of women who wore their hair this way, but she'd never actually known anyone who did so. Most of the mothers at Riley still had long hair that they pulled up in knots above their head. This woman also wore glasses, with dark round frames. "You must be a teacher," she blurted out.

The woman laughed and walked over to them. Only "walked" wasn't the right word, Willa thought; "walked" was too ordinary a description. This woman marched over, holding her hand out in front of her as though she was about to get the girls to agree to something.

"I don't know what sort of teacher I'd make," the woman said, shaking first Roselia's hand and then Willa's. "But I'm pleased to make your acquaintance. I'm Grace McCartney."

"How do you do, Miss McCartney," Willa said. Roselia only nodded, her eyes wide. At least she had managed to close her mouth.

"Please just call me Grace."

"I'm Willa, and this is Roselia." This set off another

round of shaking hands. "But my mama wouldn't like me calling you Grace. Not with you a grown woman."

"Hmmm." The woman considered this and muttered, "At least someone thinks I'm grown." Then she smiled. "Well, Miss Grace then?"

Willa couldn't help but smile back. Roselia seemed to be coming out of her spell. "Miss Grace then," her friend repeated.

The woman put an arm around each one of the girls. The white of Miss Grace's sleeves looked very bright against Willa's faded dress. "Your blouse is very pretty," Willa said, feeling a little shy. She didn't know that she'd ever seen something so crisp and new this close.

"You like it? I had a dickens of a time getting it ironed just right."

Willa tried to picture this woman standing over an ironing board, fussing over every little bit. She failed.

"I'd hoped to have these books on the shelves by nightfall, but I got a late start this morning."

Willa turned her head so quickly the world blurred. "Those are books?" she asked, pointing to the truck. She couldn't remember the number of boxes that had already been unloaded, but there were a half dozen or so still waiting. Trying to figure out the number of boxes filled with at least several books each made Willa dizzy. "Are they all yours?"

"Well, some of them are and, anyway, they were mine to bring. But it's my hope you'll make them yours. Would you like to come and see?" Stepping briskly, the woman led them to the porch where they paused to let the movers take in another load. Then they ducked inside. "How are you two about unpacking things? These folks need to get the truck back to Fairmont, but I could use some help. I'd be happy to pay . . ."

Willa stopped listening. All along the back wall, row after row, were bookshelves straight and tall as soldiers. Surely this Miss Grace didn't have books enough to fill all those shelves! But there were so many boxes, just waiting there, piled on tables and on the half dozen chairs that looked just perfect if someone were so inclined to sit and read awhile.

"There's my rug," Miss Grace was saying, her voice distant. As Willa tried to focus, the woman pointing to the corner grew small and shrunken, as though miles stretched between. "It used to be in my room when I was a little girl. I figure it might make things more comfy."

Willa's eyes darted from the shelves to the boxes to the rug and back all over again. The disappointment was so strong that she felt it washing through her mouth, a salty-sweet taste. In all her life, she'd never known so many books existed—and to think that they were right here in Riley Mines.

And Willa was leaving in the morning.

With a small cry, she turned away. "I can't," she gasped out, as though she had finished a long running race instead of being on the verge of taking flight. "I can't." And without another word, Willa fled.

Chapter Six

When Willa arrived back at the house, she found it full of unhappy people. Mama was sitting in the chair, her head bent over Rusty, silver hair loose and covering her face. Even with Mama's eyes hidden, Willa was sure that her mother had been crying. Daddy stood over by the stove, pouring a cup of coffee, which would have been normal enough, but his hand shook and Willa could hear the lid clank against the pot.

"What's going on?" Willa asked. She turned to her brother, who was sprawled in the corner, his jaw so tight that Willa was surprised she couldn't hear his teeth grinding together. She'd never seen Ves this upset before. "Mama?" she asked.

But her mother only shook her head, obviously not trusting herself to speak just yet.

Seeing Mama like this, defeated, distressed, all this

reminded Willa of those awful winter nights when she'd heard her mother crying in the darkness. A rush of fury and fear she'd tried desperately to bury deep and hide within the very heart of her own body burst like a fire, as though Willa was made of dry kindling and someone set a match to her. She turned on her brother. "What did you say to make Mama cry?" she demanded, her voice all the more scary for being low and sounding calm.

"Willa," she heard her father caution her from across the room, but she was so heavy with her own feelings that she might tip over if she stopped. Ves rose, and although Willa was shorter by a good three inches, she felt as though they were seeing each other eye to eye.

"What did you say?" she repeated.

Ves did not look away. "Mama doesn't want us to go to Hawk's Nest."

From behind, Willa heard her mother stir. "That isn't true, Ves. . . ."

"You said you won't go. And you know Daddy won't leave you here," Ves said, his voice rising. "So it's all the same thing if you ask me."

"That's enough, son," Daddy called out, his voice cracking across the room. Ves slumped against the wall of the cabin, his mouth grim.

Willa looked at her family—from Mama with Rusty, who stared with round eyes the same brown shade as

Willa's own; to Daddy with both hands clutching the coffee cup as though it were a lifeline; his last hope.

Seraphina and Kyle watched from the bedroom doorway, Sera's pretty face thin and white, as though the emotion in the room had drained the very life out of her. Kyle hid behind his sister.

There was no point in looking at Ves, Willa knew. If she did, she might let loose the anger again, and she wasn't sure she could afford to do that. For years, the Lowells had watched one family after another tear apart by the strain of living through this Depression; through the seemingly endless poverty and want that followed in its wake. For years they had seen mother turn against father, children against their parents. They'd seen brothers disrespect their sisters who in turn became vicious and bitter. Family after family had broken up, each person too beaten down to see anything other than their own desperate pain.

But never—not in all the years they had struggled through—did Willa ever think this would happen to them. Not to her family. Not to Willa.

And it won't, Willa determined. Not now. Not ever.

Willa went over to her younger sister and brother and knelt in front of them. "This ain't no place for you right now," she told them, keeping her voice as gentle as she could. "You just let us all talk it over, and I promise you I'll come and tell you what's going on as soon as I know."

Seraphina looked up, and perhaps Mama or Daddy nodded behind Willa's back, because the little girl's face smoothed out and she took a deep breath as though she'd been holding hers in for a long time. "You promise?" she asked.

"Promise," Willa said. She stood up and took them both into the other room, and shook out the straw-and-newspaper-filled ticks to make them as soft as she could manage. "If you both lie down a little while, I'll let you share the Granny quilt." When they did so without question, Willa didn't know if they were genuinely pleased by the rare treat or were just pretending to be so, but she was glad to get them tucked beneath it and settled for a few minutes. Then she went back into the front room and closed the door behind her.

"Now," Willa said. "Can we talk about this or are we just going to yell?" She glared at her brother.

Ves rubbed his hand over his head, not unlike the way Daddy did when he was upset. "I'm sorry, Mama."

To their surprise a small flutter of a smile passed over Mama's face. Then, without warning, she started to laugh. They all three stared at her, and Willa wondered if her mother hadn't gone silly. Still, Mama seemed sane enough, sitting there with Rusty bouncing on her knee.

"Did you ever think we'd raise such bossy children?" she asked her husband.

Daddy gave Mama a look so loving that Willa caught

her breath. She'd rarely seen her father that vulnerable; she could count on two hands the number of times she'd heard him tell Mama that he loved her. But no one who saw a man look at his wife like that would doubt that the feeling between them was very real. "I reckon anyone raised by you, Esther, would have an independence streak."

"That they do," Mama said, smiling up at both of them as though they were the most terrific children in the world. But then she got her twitching mouth under control and pointed from one to the other, the way she reprimanded Sera and Kyle. "I think you and you," she said, "had better be sitting down so we can talk this through. If you're old enough to think you can tell us what to do, then you're old enough to listen. Your daddy and I have been on this earth a bit longer than you both combined, and what you got in enthusiasm I hope to heaven your father and I make up in wisdom."

Willa leaned back against the wall and slowly slid down, feeling the rough wood of the cabin pluck like fingers against the threads of her dress. All of the fight had gone out of her in as sudden a whoosh as it had come. Now that Mama and Daddy were so clearly back in charge, she found that the nervousness she'd been keeping within her had moved to just beneath her skin. She felt twitchy with it, her fingers and toes wanting to tap upon the wooden floor like a drum.

"I think the best thing for us all would be for Ves and

Daddy to go to Hawk's Nest and leave the rest of us here." Mama looked at her oldest son. "I wish I could do more, Ves, but I can't. I haven't the strength." Her words were so steady that they seemed to belie what she was saying.

"I've no intention of leaving you—," Daddy began, but Mama held up her hand.

"It ain't about you leaving, it's about you going."

"What about the house?" Ves asked. "If the mines open and one of us ain't here to work, the guards might set you out."

Willa hadn't thought of that, and this fear joined the chorus of worry that beat within her belly. She could feel it as steady as the cold and hunger all last winter had been.

"We'll deal with that when the time comes," Mama answered. "If it comes. The guards do seem to be more eager to drink and carry on than bothering with the likes of us who keep the peace."

Ves paced back and forth, as though only the walls kept him from leaving that very minute. He can't wait to go, Willa realized. He was eighteen after all. At eighteen, Daddy had been on his own. At eighteen, Mama had been married. Even if he doesn't leave now, she thought, he will soon. And in less than two years, Willa would be eighteen too. Would she be so eager?

"I could get Johnny Settle to make sure the coal bin

was kept full," he said. "We was talking about everything earlier today."

Willa knew this meant that Johnny would likely steal it from the mines—not in a big way or anything; the coal was often low-grade to begin with, hacked from a seam too small for the company to bother with. And each family only took what they needed, just around the edges. Still, she felt a little sick, thinking that they would ask someone to be a thief. There has to be a better way, but if there was, she couldn't figure it out.

Daddy shook his head. "I've already said I won't go without you."

Mama reached out and he took her hand in his, holding it delicately as if it was infinitely precious. The certainty on his weathered face crumpled about the edges. "You're not leaving me, Wait," she told him softly. "You're doing your best for your family. And to tell you the truth, I'm not sure we have any other choice."

Willa remembered what Daddy had said in town that afternoon—a man's always got a choice. But did they?

"After all, Willa's nearly grown." Mama turned to her and smiled. "She's been a wonderful help to me this whole past year. I never would have made it through without her."

Daddy bit his lip; Willa knew he was torn.

"We'll be fine, Daddy," she said, bolstered by her

mother's praise. But even so, Willa couldn't help but feel that with Daddy and Ves gone anything might happen—that if she let them out of her sight, they might disappear into the yawning nothingness that was the Depression. But if Mama could be brave, if Daddy and Ves could find the strength to go without them, then Willa couldn't bear to let them all down.

For nearly an hour they talked it out, and Willa noticed that the more times they told each other that everything would be fine, the easier the words became to say. The family came together and began to plan what should be packed, what could be taken. What tools were too heavy and which were necessary? Would they both need a pick, or only one? Well over an hour had passed before Willa guiltily remembered her promise to Sera and Kyle. When she opened the door, she saw her brother had fallen asleep, although Seraphina was still waiting, some of the color back in her cheeks.

"I listened at the door," Sera admitted. "Not because I didn't trust you to come, but just I wanted to know how, well, how to be, when you told us what was going to happen."

Willa could feel tears pricking her eyes, and she reached out and hugged her sister close, feeling the very bones of the girl. I should do this more often, she scolded herself, wishing her words of pride could find a way from her tight throat. Perhaps the unexpected hug would be enough; it would tell Sera how much she meant even if her tongue could not.

Somehow the family got through the rest of the day; though they all worked together, Willa wondered if everyone else felt the loneliness she did. If so, no one mentioned it. Willa and Mama washed and ironed clothes, folding them with great concentration as though by smoothing them with their hands they might somehow keep their menfolk safe with their soon-to-be-distant touch. Ves let Kyle help him pack the bags; Sera brushed Daddy's hat until the felt shone with her efforts. Daddy patched his and Ves's shoes with cardboard, and lined them with the last of the newspaper from Mr. Olivetti. Willa baked potatoes and cornbread, both of which would be filling and easy to eat with their fingers from the back of a truck. At supper, no one did more than pick at the meal, so Willa packed the rest of that food too.

All during the preparations, Mama joked and told stories about her childhood on the farm—including one of Willa's favorites, about the time she'd been picking berries and stood on an anthill. Mama jumped about the room shaking her leg as though the ants were crawling on her still. Willa laughed along with everyone else.

But that night, after the younger children had gone to bed and Mama and Daddy were settling in for the night, Willa left the house and headed up the mountain to the pioneer cabin. The stars would be bright tonight, and perhaps she could stare up at them and remember that no matter where Daddy and Ves went, they would all look up at the same glittering sky.

Unlike the night in October when she'd gone with Ves, this time she went by herself; this time she did not ask permission.

No one stopped her. No one asked where she was going. And Willa knew that this was Mama and Daddy's way of telling her without using words that they trusted her.

Since she was Seraphina's age, Willa had dreamed of what it would feel like, being grown up. Now that she'd arrived, she wasn't sure. She certainly didn't feel any different; she was still Willa Lowell of Riley Mines. But all around there were changes being made, starting inside of her.

Now Willa walked alone.

Chapter Seven

After Daddy and Ves had gone, the Lowell house grew quiet. Willa knew that days would pass before a letter from Ves could be expected, and the wait dragged so long that her very muscles ached from it. Mama tried to talk in her cheerful way about what they must be seeing or doing, but Willa could not be distracted from the image of the two men huddled in the back of an open truck; a group of ragged men traveling farther and farther from the people they loved.

In this strange new hush, Seraphina seemed to grow louder, more fierce. Not a day—often not even an afternoon—went by where she didn't manage to run into something, knock something off kilter, or somehow manage to shatter something into pieces, always doing so with the most possible noise, or so it sounded to Willa.

"Can't you be more careful?" Willa demanded when

her sister dropped a stack of tin plates to the floor with a crash. Willa's patience was at an end: just that morning Sera'd been jumping rope on the front porch, cracking one of the flimsy floorboards and leaving a hole Willa didn't know how to fix.

"They were too hot," Sera told her, picking them up at the rim, the dishtowel so threadbare you could see the silver metal shining through it. Willa knew it didn't offer the small hands much protection. But this was just one of a long string of endless accidents.

"Now we have to wash them again," Willa complained.

Seraphina blew on one of the plates. "There. Looks clean to me."

"It ain't and you know it," Willa yelled, trying to convince herself that she wouldn't have done the same if Seraphina hadn't been so annoying about it.

"You're just being bossy," Seraphina said, turning around so quickly that she banged into the table, the sharp corner biting into the soft part of her stomach. "Ow!" she shrieked.

In the other room, Rusty began to cry.

"Now see what you've done?" Willa hissed.

Mama opened the door and peered out. "What's going on out there?"

"Nothing," the two said together, each trying not to glare at the other. Willa shoved the plates, dusty or not, on the small shelf by the stove. Sera rubbed her stomach.

Mama didn't look convinced, but she didn't scold. "If you've finished the dishes, you might go down into town for a few minutes. Or take a walk. We've all been a little cooped up around here the past few days."

"Come on, Sera," Willa said. She'd rather go down to Riley alone, but even taking her sister was better than staying inside. The two headed down the hill, running with their unexpected freedom.

"Where are we going?" Seraphina asked when they reached the main road.

"I want to go over to the missionary building," Willa said, turning right.

"Well, I want to go to the creek," Sera said, stamping her foot so hard that the mud from the rain that morning oozed between her toes.

Willa sighed. "We'll be filthy in five minutes." Sera crossed her arms. "Okay, the Mission first, then the creek."

When they arrived at the old storefront, Willa could not believe how different the place had become in only a few days time. The outside was painted a greenish-blue with maroon trim around the windows and the door. These colors, Willa realized, wouldn't show the coal dust the way lighter shades would, yet were still fresh and bright looking. Why didn't they paint the houses like this instead of whitewashing? In contrast to the boarded windows of the company store, the operator houses, and the mining office, the big pane of glass across the front of the Mission sparkled. The whole building seemed to stand up taller, as though it knew just how important it looked against the rest of the shuttered town.

"Are you sure we're allowed to go in there?" Seraphina asked, some of her bravado fading.

"I'm sure," Willa said, although she wasn't.

Just then a woman came out and called to them, "Willa? Is that you?"

Willa gasped. They'd only met the woman for a few moments last week. How had she remembered her name? Known who she was even yards away? Not that Willa had forgotten Miss Grace's name, but it seemed almost impossible to believe that the well-dressed stranger could have recalled hers.

Miss Grace walked out into the street, and soon had put her arms around them just as she had Willa and Roselia before. "I was hoping you'd come back," she said. "And who did you bring with you?"

"She's my sister," Willa said.

"I'm Sera," the little girl added. "Short for Seraphina, not like Sarah in the Bible."

"I'm glad to meet you, Sera-short-for-Seraphina-not-like-Sarah-in-the-Bible," Miss Grace said.

Sera giggled.

The three of them moved off the street and stood outside the door of the Mission. "Have you come to get a book?" Miss Grace asked them. "I have some wonderful ones: *Little Women, Five Little Peppers and How They Grew, Anne of Green Gables* . . ."

The younger girl's interest began to wander, even as Willa's reached a fever pitch.

"I'm not much of a reader," Sera said, sounding almost proud.

Willa couldn't stand it. "That's because you don't try," she said, not bothering to hide her anger. "Even when they open the school, you don't bother going half the time. Not unless Mama makes you." Here she was, longing for a chance to go to school and Seraphina didn't even care.

"I'm the pretty one in the family," Sera told Miss Grace. "Willa's the smart one."

"You both look pretty smart to me," Miss Grace said with a wink, and Sera giggled again. Miss Grace is an awful lot like Mama, Willa decided, the way she jokes with us, taking the sting out of things. But this evidently wasn't enough for Sera, who was tugging on Willa's arm.

"You said we could go to the creek."

"In a minute," Willa said. She could see inside the doorway to the walls lined with books—more books than she'd ever seen before in her entire life. Last week she'd torn herself away, but she couldn't do it again—not after she'd come this close.

"You said—"

"I said in a minute." Willa envisioned her sister in the Mission—the tables falling over and books tumbling from the shelves as though she pulled them loose with an invisible net. The whole place would be in shambles in a few minutes. Still, Willa could not leave. Reluctantly taking her eyes from the books she turned to Seraphina and tried to look stern. "Can I trust you to go to the creek?" she asked. Willa knew that Mama wouldn't approve, but she was sure that Sera would be pleased to have a secret; assuming, of course, that she could keep one. "You promise to stay on the banks and not to wade in or anything like that? The water's still too cold and the last thing we need is sickness in the house."

"I promise," Seraphina said.

"You won't leave till I come get you?"

"Fine." The little girl dashed off.

Miss Grace stared after her with a slight frown upon her face. After a moment, she turned back to Willa, her smile as broad as ever. "Would you like to see the books?" she asked.

"Yes, ma'am," Willa answered, her voice almost a whisper.

Even with the bright electric lights burning overhead,

the room inside the Mission was dim after the bright sun outside. Nothing in the room was new—the stuffed furniture was shiny in places, but in all the *right* places, just where she herself would put an elbow or tuck up a dangling foot. The tables were nicked about the edges, but that only meant they had held many objects in their time and were eager to hold more. The rug on the floor was worn in spots, as though letting Willa know it was all ready for her to step upon it.

"I got in a lovely copy of *Little Women*," Miss Grace said, going over and pulling a book from the shelves. When she held it out Willa couldn't help but notice that it wasn't only the book that was lovely but also the woman's smooth, soft hands. Had she been offered anything other than a book, Willa would have hidden her own grubby, work-worn ones behind her back. Instead, she reached out.

She could tell it was brand new—had never been read by anyone ever before. The cover crackled when she opened it. The pages were bright-white clean and smelled so good that Willa put the book to her nose.

Miss Grace laughed.

Willa was so ashamed of being childish that she almost dropped the book and ran away. But then Miss Grace bent down and sniffed the book herself. "Don't you just love the way a new book smells?" she asked.

"Yes, ma'am," Willa answered. She didn't want to admit that this was the first new book she had ever seen.

Miss Grace studied Willa—a frank, friendly gaze that Willa found herself returning. "You don't have to call me 'ma'am,' all the time. I would like to be your friend, and you don't call your friends 'ma'am,' now do you?"

"No ma'am . . ." Willa started to answer then caught herself. She didn't mind a bit when Miss Grace hugged her. They were soon sitting in the big soft chairs, the new book between them.

For over an hour they read together, Miss Grace helping Willa sound out the words she didn't always understand. Miss Grace explained things too—how Mr. March was off fighting in the Civil War between North and South, for starters. So much of the world of *Little Women* was strange to Willa.

"You mean you never had presents at Christmas?" Miss Grace asked after they read the passage about the March girls finding gifts beneath their pillows.

Willa shook her head. "Used to be the coal company handed out an orange and a bag of candy to each child, but they ain't done that since before Kyle was born. I doubt if Seraphina even remembers." She paused a minute. "And there are the stories Mama tells, from back on the farm she grew up on; about shooting off rifles and hearing the shots round the valley."

Miss Grace nodded. "They do that where I come from too, and it's a lot of fun."

"Mama used to tell me about putting greens in the windows and mistletoe over the doors. And the big breakfasts everyone had, like the March girls give away." Willa shook her head, unable to quite put her world and that of the March sisters together. "I don't think even Mama ever had anything as fancy as what Mr. Laurence gave the March sisters."

"Mr. Laurence was something special, all right," Miss Grace said. Willa, though she said nothing, thought he sounded a little like a coal operator, with his big house and pots of money he spent mostly on himself.

"My mama grew up on a farm, so I guess I just always figured that Christmas was part of farming life."

"But you're a coal mine girl, aren't you?" Miss Grace asked.

Maybe Miss Grace thought her babyish after all. "I'm sixteen, you know," Willa said, her voice a little stiff.

Miss Grace seemed to understand and thought a minute. "A miner's daughter?" she asked.

Willa liked the sound of that: she'd always be a daughter, no matter how old she grew. "My daddy says I cut my eyeteeth on a coal tipple."

Miss Grace's green eyes lit up and Willa wondered if everything gleamed so in the electric lights, much brighter than the coal oil lamp or stubby candle the Lowells used. "I don't believe anyone cuts her eyeteeth on a tipple. Open your mouth and let me see." That sounded like a dare!

Reveling in the silliness, Willa opened as wide as she could. Miss Grace rose to the challenge and peered deep into Willa's mouth.

"You must have done a good job," Miss Grace said, her voice echoing a bit inside of Willa. "I don't see eyes in any of your teeth."

Willa giggled, feeling as young as Seraphina for a moment. "Eyeteeth," she said. "I'll have to tell Ves about that." But then she remembered that he was gone and the giddiness fell away, leaving the weight of responsibility in its place.

"Have you ever been to your mama's farm?" asked Miss Grace.

"No ma—" Willa caught herself. "No. It's all the way over in Marion County. Mama never even gets to go, not even when Aunt Margaret was married last year."

"Marion County's my home," Miss Grace said. "I grew up in Fairmont. It's not so far away that you couldn't go and visit every once in a while."

Willa shook her head. "Then I must be getting the names mixed up. Mama said it was real far to go."

Miss Grace bit her lip. "Your mama is probably right."

"I've never even been outside of Riley," Willa said, "let alone all the way to Marion County."

"You know, I wanted to go away to Africa and be a missionary," Miss Grace said. "When I was your age, I read a book about a woman over in Africa and as soon as I closed the covers, I knew that was what I wanted to do with my life."

"Is Riley Mines in Africa?" Willa asked.

Miss Grace looked amazed. "Riley is in West Virginia, Willa. In the United States, not Africa."

"Oh," Willa said. She felt stupid, not knowing where Africa was. "Is Africa as far away as Mama's farm? Or is it really far, like Italy, where the Olivettis came from?" Roselia had often told tales about her parents coming on a big boat to New York and making their way to the coal mines. There were plenty of hair-raising stories of deaths, or at least, near misses—Roselia relished the idea that if either of her parents had been sent back that neither she nor Theresa would be alive.

"Let me show you something," Miss Grace said. Willa could hear the soothing sound of skirts rustling across Miss Grace's chair as she stood. She followed Miss Grace over to the wall, where there was a big picture painted pale blue, with funny shapes in lots of different colors.

"This is a map of the world," Miss Grace said. She pointed to a pink shape, where Willa could make out the words "United States of America" written across it. "You and I"—she picked up a pencil and made a dot on the pink—"are just about here."

Willa looked at the dot. It looked so small on the huge picture. "Where's Africa?" she asked.

"Over here," Miss Grace said, gesturing. "Across the Atlantic Ocean."

Compared to the dot Miss Grace had made in the United States, Africa was huge. Bigger even than the whole pink United States. It was filled with shapes that looked like autumn leaves scattered on the ground up on the mountain.

Willa stared at the map, trying to sound out the words, Miss Grace helping her with "Mexico," a fun word to say, and "Asia," which sounded mysterious. "Italy is here," Miss Grace said, pointing. "It's part of Europe."

"Roselia will want to see this," Willa said, pleased that this time she would be the one bringing news to her friend instead of the other way around. "Where is Mama's farm?"

"Marion County is right about here," Miss Grace said. She took the pencil and drew another circle, just below the first circle she had drawn.

"That's not far at all," Willa said. "Not like Africa or Italy."

"Not nearly so far."

"Was that why you came here instead of Africa? It was too far away?"

"Well, I guess that's as good a reason as any," Miss Grace said. "My daddy felt I should do my missionary work at home."

"Are you gonna preach?" Willa asked. Mama and Daddy weren't very happy with the company minister, but Willa rather thought Miss Grace would be a terrific preacher.

Miss Grace shook her head. "I'm not going to preach."

"Then why are you here?" Willa asked. She looked around the room, where the shelves were filled with books and the walls were covered with pictures of animals and plants.

"Just to help," Miss Grace said.

Willa did not know what to say. She had never known someone who wanted to help for no reason; at least not for a reason that people would understand: being family or close friends.

When she turned from the map, Willa was startled to see that the sun had started to go down—with the bright electric lights, she hadn't even noticed. Mama was probably worried sick, wondering where they'd gone. "I gotta go get my sister," she told Miss Grace. "Thank you for telling me about Africa."

"Thank you for listening," Miss Grace said. "Would

you like to take this home with you and work on it?" She picked up *Little Women*.

"No, ma'am," Willa answered before she could remember that she wasn't supposed to call Miss Grace "ma'am." "I mean, it's too pretty and new. I don't want to dirty it."

Miss Grace pushed the book closer. Willa could see the white pages between the dark covers. She caught another whiff of new book smell, as fragrant to her as any perfume.

"You take it, Willa. It's nice to have new books, I know, but books are written to be read. I'm sure you'll be careful."

Willa took the book in both hands. She thought about how delightful it would be to read when the house was quiet. Maybe Mama would like to hear her read out loud. If she was very careful not to splash, Willa could read as she did the laundry, or the supper dishes. Even if she couldn't get down to Miss Grace's new library soon, she would still have this book for a few days.

"Thank you," Willa said. Then she turned and ran out the door just in case Miss Grace changed her mind and took the book away.

When she reached the edge of the creek, she found Seraphina waiting for her on the bank. Her face and hands muddy, the little girl acted as innocent and pleasant as could be, but Willa noted the damp rim about the skirt of her dress and knew that her sister, as usual, had paid no attention to Willa's fears and done as she pleased. No doubt she'd waded in the icy waters of the creek the entire time, coming out only when she heard her sister's footsteps on the path.

All that night, Willa waited to hear her sister begin to cough, to sneeze. But Seraphina slept through the entire night, without so much as snoring. Perhaps, Willa hoped, they'd finally had a little luck.

Just before dawn, a very tired Willa took her book out to the kitchen and lit a candle. Soon Mama and the younger children would be up and the day would begin, but for a few minutes at least, there was time to read.

Chapter Eight

Over a week passed before the first letter from Ves arrived. Only a short, penciled note, as much scrawl as could be called handwriting, Ves told them that he and Daddy had arrived at Hawk's Nest safely. "There is work for those who can do it. Pay not great, but it's steady. Send our love."

"Blessed be," Mama murmured when she heard it, and some of the fine, weblike lines on her forehead smoothed out.

Tucked inside the note were two one-dollar bills, which Mama put carefully in a crockery jar. She kept the letter itself close by and from time to time asked Willa if she wouldn't mind reading it again.

As happy as she was about the letter, Willa couldn't stop thinking about the money. It had been so long since she'd actually seen a real dollar bill that Willa longed simply to touch them. At night, she and Seraphina would lie in bed and whisper about what they would like to buy, now that there was money to spend. The company store was open several days each month, and Seraphina drooled over the food: the dressed rabbits that hung in the window; the golden wheels of cheese; the pickles and sauerkraut kept in barrels bigger than Kyle was high. "You think they'll still have grapes, like they did last year?" she asked, her voice wistful. "You know the kind with the sawdust still on them? Bet they'd taste mighty good."

"Hard to imagine anyone in Riley Mines able to afford grapes," Willa said. "Guards, maybe. They're the only ones working. 'Cept for people like Daddy and Ves, sending money back." Having money was a physical pleasure; even a few dollars in the house made her feel safer than she had since last fall. "I used to wonder why they bothered opening at all, it seemed so mean. I walked by and told myself it was better not to even go in, and see all those things I couldn't buy. Now, with a bit of cash money, won't it be grand to go shopping again?"

"Yeah." Seraphina rolled over with a contented sigh, the thin mattress rustling beneath her.

Unlike her sister, Willa didn't think about food—she kept imagining the clothes she could have. Her dress from last fall had been repaired (the sleeve a different color that looked just dreadful), but when Daddy had talked about Willa having something new, she'd let herself dream about the lovely red cotton cloth tucked away on the top shelf, over by the tinware. Surely, with the mines closed, no one had been able to buy it; Willa could practically hear the swishing sound of scissors cutting—maybe Mama would make her a middy blouse with a white lawn tie.

But when they asked Mama what they would spend the money on, they were dismayed to learn that Mama didn't plan to spend it at all.

"Well, we'll have to spend a little something," she said as they all walked down into town together. "I'd like to get some milk for Kyle and Rusty, and a glass for Sera wouldn't do her any harm." (Willa noticed that her sister hadn't asked for coffee since election day.) "We'll get some soup beans, and more cornmeal." Perhaps the disappointment Willa felt showed on her face, because Mama wrinkled her own nose in sympathy. "I will admit to being sick to death of cornbread, though."

Once inside the store, it was even harder to resist. Jars of gumdrops and licorice strips sat tantalizingly close to the counter edge. The air was scented with peppermint and hot roasted peanuts. "It's best to save what we can," Mama reminded them. "We don't know yet what's to come." When she put a penny into each of their hands, it was hard not to feel disappointed.

Then Willa chuckled.

"What is it?" Seraphina asked.

"If anyone would have told me a month ago I'd be sad about getting only a penny for a treat, I'd have called them crazy."

Sera looked down at her copper coin. Then she grinned back at her sister. "You're right."

While Mama bought supplies, the two went carefully over the sweets and penny candy. Sera decided on a chocolate bar, though she was torn between that and the oval-shaped tea cookies. Willa chose a bag of lemon drops. "They're so sour, you can't eat more than one—that makes them last," she said, her mouth puckering.

On the way home, Willa saw Miss Grace coming across the street. When the missionary saw them, she came right over.

"You must be Mrs. Lowell," she said, holding out her hand. "Willa I already know," she said, tipping her head, then she winked. "And Sera-as-in-Seraphina too."

The playfulness made Mama smile. She shifted Rusty to her other arm and shook Miss Grace's hand. "And you must be Willa's Miss Grace," she said. "The older boy is my son Kyle, and the little 'un is Rusty."

"Hello, Kyle. Hello, Rusty." She shook hands with the little boy and even the baby, and then looked again at Mrs. Lowell. "Would you have a moment to take a cup of tea over at the Mission? I've been meaning to call but I had to go back to Fairmont last week unexpectly." Although Mama hadn't agreed, they all began to walk toward the old store-front. "I understand you're from Marion County also?"

Mama nodded. "My folks had a place out past Farmington. I grew up there."

"Well, I'll be," Miss Grace said. "My uncle used to be a minister there, at the Methodist church. The one on the corner, right in downtown."

"Yes, I know just the one you mean," Mama said. They had reached the Mission and Miss Grace pushed the button to turn on the electric lights. When Mama saw all the books, she glanced at Willa. "I can see why you're always asking to come visit." Mama sounded a little nervous. Not even the talk about Marion County had set her completely at ease.

"Your daughter is a wonderful reader," Miss Grace said. "I hope she'll enjoy many more of the books we have."

Mama glanced around the room. "If there's any way we can repay you for letting Willa borrow them, I'd be happy to."

Miss Grace shook her head. "Not at all. It's not unlike a lending library—you know, the kind they have in cities? You can borrow the books for free; that's what they're there for."

Willa could see that Mama didn't know, but all she said was, "Well, I know Willa would help you out, any way she could. And you only have to say the word, and I'll do what I can."

For a moment, Willa held her breath. Ever since she'd met Miss Grace, Willa had figured the two women were more alike than not—the way they laughed, the way they made you feel better just by being with them. But in her faded dress, clean and tidy though it was, with safety pins holding closed the places where the buttons had gone missing, Mama and the woman next to her in the starched white blouse and dark blue skirt couldn't have looked more different. With her glasses and shiny shoes, would Miss Grace notice how special Mama was? Would her new friend understand just how much it meant to Mama to be able to offer something, even if it was only a chance to do some chores?

But she needn't have worried. Miss Grace reached out and touched Mama gently on the arm. "I'll keep that in mind, Mrs. Lowell. I'm much obliged."

Then they all had tea in pretty china cups, even Seraphina, with milk in jelly glasses for the little boys. From the back, Miss Grace brought out a plate of cookies—the same ones Sera had longed for back at the company store. Willa watched as her sister took only one, leaving two for Kyle. Perhaps Miss Grace noticed too, because when the cookies were gone, she went back for more.

After that, Willa seemed to have more and more time to run down the hill and take part in all the Mission had to offer. Ves evidently had made good on his promise to ask his friend Johnny to keep the coal bin full, because Willa never went out and found it empty. Just as Willa had slowly taken over the household chores last fall, now that Mama was able to do to more, she lifted many of those burdens one by one from Willa's shoulders, all without saying a word.

Sometimes Roselia went with her, and sometimes Seraphina and Theresa tagged along, although neither of the younger girls was interested in hanging around while their older sisters read. Not that you were required to sit and be still; every week Miss Grace tried to offer something new, something worth learning that was also fun. Once she brought a treadle sewing machine and taught them all how to sew a seam by making handkerchiefs, which Miss Grace then embroidered with each girl's initials. Willa loved hers—it was pale blue, with dark blue stitches saying *WLL* for Willa Laura Lowell. "Your initials are almost like your name," Miss Grace said. "And I love the way all those *L*'s just roll off the tongue."

Willa had never sounded out her whole name before, but she, too, liked the way it sounded when she said the whole thing. Willa Laura Lowell. She imagined going into a post office, or even the company store, where telegrams were sent and received. "Anything for Willa Laura Lowell?"

she would ask. Why, she could be anyone at all, someone important, with a name like that.

Not all the sewing was fancy; by the end of the week every dress had been patched and sewn, the hems and cuffs let out as far as they could go to cover bony knees and knobby wrists. Skirts handed down but not yet grown into were taken in, the bands of extra fabric used to shape a new collar, or a pretty belt. Willa's mismatched dress looked worse than ever.

Boys joined in on the hot June day Miss Grace borrowed a truck and took more than twenty of them to an old abandoned farm where wild strawberries grew in the thickets about the barn and tumbledown house. Even when they returned and the cooking pots came out, the boys helped carry bag after bag of white cane sugar while the girls cooked the berries into jam. Everyone, boys and girls alike, carried home a jar.

"It's too pretty to eat," Roselia said, holding hers up to the light and letting the sun shine through it. "It's like a church window."

"I'd put a window on corn bread if it made it taste any better," Willa said, wishing not for the first time that summer for a taste of yeast bread or a hot roll. She didn't say anything to Roselia about the money hidden in the crock, but she enjoyed remembering it was there. Once, when Mama and the others had gone to sleep, Willa had crept over and taken the savings out, counting the bills by feel in the darkness. There were more than thirty, and the thickness of them in her hand more than made up for the days of worry she had endured last winter.

Roselia might have been able to save her jam, but Mama used up Willa's that very night. She sliced across a pan of corn bread, spreading the sweetness between the layers. When she cut it, she made pie-shaped slivers instead of squares. "It's almost like cake, isn't it?" she said.

Willa rolled her eyes but played along, using her fork (whoever heard of eating corn bread with a fork?). To her surprise, Mama was right—the jam made all the difference.

The Mission was always busy. Nearly every night after supper a few of them gathered beneath the bright electric lights and enjoyed the books. Sometimes Miss Grace read aloud, but other times she would be busy combing out a child's hair and asked to listen as she worked. Willa knew by the way Miss Grace used a different comb for each person, and then carefully dipped the comb into coal oil before wiping it clean, that she was removing lice. At first Willa was ashamed—would Miss Grace think they all had bugs in their hair? Mama would just die if she thought someone thought that about any of her children. And then there was the day when Alice Anker came; the Ankers had one of the dirtiest cabins in all of Riley Mines and Willa could see the smattering of bites from fleas and bedbugs clustered like red stars over the girl's bare legs.

Miss Grace didn't seem to pay any attention. "Willa is reading to us from *Treasure Island*. Would you like to join us?" Alice nodded and sat down. A few days later she was sitting under Miss Grace's comb and left with a pink satin ribbon in her hair that Willa figured would be filthy within the hour. But when she saw Alice a week later the ribbon still shone. "I wash the tie every night," she said, patting her greasy hair.

Willa shuddered. Maybe Miss Grace could stand it, but Willa couldn't. When she mentioned it, all Miss Grace said was, "Not everyone has a mother like your mama." When Alice didn't come back, Miss Grace marched right up to the door of the filthy place and asked for her.

The most wonderful moments were the times Willa and Miss Grace sat and read together after everyone else had gone home. Although Willa had read many novels that summer, both in the Mission and back at home, she still felt a little odd reading about girls who went to parties like the March sisters, or had ice-cream socials, like Anne Shirley of Green Gables.

"I know that they didn't have easy lives," Willa told Miss Grace. "I mean, Anne was an orphan and I'm lucky that way. But it just seems too different somehow."

"How so?" Miss Grace asked.

Willa tried to find the right way to say what she was

thinking. "Well, the words are all there, but they don't seem to mean anything."

Miss Grace looked puzzled. "I'm not sure I understand. Do the books confuse you in some way?"

"Sometimes," Willa said, embarrassed. She hoped Miss Grace wouldn't think she was complaining. She couldn't bear a life without the books, even if she didn't always like them. "I don't really know what I mean. Or I do, but I can't explain it. I know what the words say, and I know what the story means, but, well, it doesn't mean what I think it should."

Tapping her fingers against her mouth, a sign, Willa knew, that her friend was thinking, Miss Grace walked over to the wall of books and took a small, thin volume from the top shelf. She flipped through the pages, glancing at one and then dismissing it for another. Finally she stopped and sat back down. "Let's try this, just to see if this helps. It's a poem, not a novel. It's 'Eldorado' by a writer named Edgar Allan Poe."

"What does 'Eldor'"—the word tripped awkwardly on Willa's tongue—"'Eldorado' mean?"

"It's Spanish, I think," Miss Grace said. "For perfect place." She began to read:

> *"Gaily bedight,*
> *A gallant knight,*
> *In sunshine and in shadow,*

Had journeyed long,
Singing a song,
In search of Eldorado.

"But he grew old—
This knight so bold—
And o'er his heart a shadow
Fell, as he found
No spot of ground
That looked like Eldorado."

From her chair, Willa could feel her skin prickle. It was like the time Ves and Mama and Daddy had been arguing over who, if any of them, should go to Hawk's Nest. Only this time, it wasn't a bad feeling—not at all—but a delicious shiver that ran up and down her spine.

"And, as his strength
Failed him at length,
He met a pilgrim shadow—
'Shadow,' said he,
'Where can it be—
This land of Eldorado?'

"'Over the Mountains
Of the Moon,

Down the Valley of the Shadow,
    Ride, boldly ride,'
    The shade replied—
    'If you seek for Eldorado.'"

When Miss Grace had finished, Willa could barely move. "Can . . . can I see it?" she asked. Without speaking, Miss Grace handed over the book. Her voice so low that she felt herself reading more than heard with her ears, Willa read over the poem again. When she reached the end she had the strangest feeling—the twitchiness was still there, but side by side was a deep sadness that was also sweet; she could burst into tears at the slightest sound.

"It's kind of funny," she said slowly, lifting her eyes from the page. "I mean, it's not as easy to read as a story is, and there are things about it that I can't claim to understand, but it means something to me." Pictures of her own mountain with the stone walls of the pioneer cabin flashed inside her mind.

Still quiet, Miss Grace nodded.

"There's a place," Willa said, her thoughts swirling around her like maple seeds. "Up on the mountain. I go there sometimes. When it gets too hard."

"I have such places too," Miss Grace whispered.

Willa looked down at the book. "He never finds it, does he? His perfect place?"

"We don't know," Miss Grace said. "The poem doesn't say."

"He could be searching, then; still looking for it?" Though she didn't mean to ask, the words came out a question.

"I wish I knew, Willa."

Willa studied Miss Grace; she had chewed her lower lip, making it redder than the upper one. The bright color matched the spots that blossomed over each cheek; behind her glasses, the usually calm dark eyes shimmered. Miss Grace wants to cry too, Willa realized. Like me, she wants him to keep looking, because she is searching too. But what on earth could Miss Grace hope to find here in Riley Mines?

"May I borrow this?" Willa asked.

"Of course," her friend answered.

As Willa walked back up the hill, she whispered the lines again. She hurried, for she couldn't wait to read the poem again, ten times, a hundred times even. It's only words, she told herself, but her racing heart knew they were much more. It was like the letters they received from time to time from Ves—no more than a few lines at best, but the family clung to them hard, as if by doing so they could clutch their men in their arms. Words are powerful. Willa had known this since that night she'd gone with Ves up on the mountain to talk about Mama. But now she realized just how powerful words could be when they were written down for someone else to read. Even when the words aren't about something real. Eldorado might not be a place you could go, but the journey of the knight was true enough.

The Lowell cabin was dark and quiet when Willa went in. As she pulled her nightgown over her head and slipped in next to Seraphina, Willa listed all of the words she heard every day in Riley Mines: Miss Grace's thoughts, Mama's stories, Roselia's tales. Someone should write them down, Willa said to herself. Someone needs to make them true.

Chapter Nine

W hat do you think?" Willa asked. She and Roselia stood in the spare room of Miss Grace's house in Fairmont. There was so much to see at once that Willa's eyes didn't know where to begin: the wallpaper decked with roses, the beds covered with lacy white spreads, even the lampshades were rippled and covered with netting so fine it fluttered when you passed by.

"I think it's like something out of a novel," Willa said. Even the floors were beautiful—the thick carpets felt like moss beneath her bare toes. She'd read in books about characters pinching themselves to make certain they were awake, and Willa did so now. Talking Mama into the trip to Fairmont hadn't been easy—not until Miss Grace had mentioned that they would visit Mama's sister, Willa's Aunt Margaret, had Mama come around. "I feel like I'm in a story."

Roselia rolled her eyes. "You think everything is about a book." She walked over to the dresser and ran her finger over the shiny wood. "And aren't you reading a book about a man stuck on an island somewhere? That's nothing like this."

"I didn't mean *Robinson Crusoe*," Willa said. "It's more like, well, I sort of feel like Alice, down in the rabbit hole."

"I think it's more like a picture show!" Roselia said.

Willa laughed. "At least I've read the novels I talk about. When did you ever see a picture show?"

Roselia grinned back at her. "Well, it's what I imagine a picture show to look like." On the dresser was a silver hairbrush that glittered in the sunlight streaming in from the many windows. "Do you think it's real?" Roselia asked. She picked it up and tried to run it through her hair, but it was too snarled and the brush caught on the curls. "Help me," she squealed to Willa.

"You shouldn't have meddled," Willa chided, trying to untangle her friend from the stiff bristles. The long strands seemed to be wound in such a way that she had to pull it free little by little.

"I'm sorry," Roselia said. Glancing at the mirror in front of them, Willa could see Roselia's eyes were filled with tears. "I didn't think."

Made guilty by those eyes, Willa spoke in a gentle voice. "I don't think Miss Grace would have put the brush here if she didn't want us to use it." She plucked the last strands free and the brush fell away. Roselia rubbed her head and scowled into the mirror. Even with Roselia frowning, her hair tangled worse than ever, Willa could see how pretty her friend was. Her dark hair and eyes and red, red mouth made Willa appear quite washed out in comparison. Willa put her hand to her own brown hair that hung limp around her shoulders and tried to fluff it, but it stayed flat. Here in this gorgeous room, beside her lovely friend, she suddenly felt that everything about her was faded and worn. Even the new blouse Mama had made for her—well, it wasn't new exactly. Mama had made it over from one of her own, but at least it wasn't the patchwork dress. The collar was stiff and bright, but she still had *coal camp* written all over her here in Fairmont. Roselia wasn't dressed any better than she was, but Willa thought the nicer hair made a big difference.

There was a tap at the door and both girls spun around. Willa dropped the hairbrush and hurried to pick it up, making things worse when it clattered on the dresser. But Miss Grace didn't seem to notice. "Are you two settling in all right?"

"Yes, ma'am," they answered without thinking.

"You make me feel like my mother," Miss Grace muttered, casting a wary eye down the hall. "And speaking of that, she just told me that dinner would be in about an hour. I want to show you where the bathroom is, so you can wash up." They followed her out of the room and into the long hallway that led to the many bedrooms in the house. Willa would have liked to peek into each one, but felt too shy to ask. The hallway itself was fancy enough— there were electric lights in the shape of bells hanging from the ceiling and a long strip of maroon carpet running down the middle.

But when she saw the bathroom, Willa could not believe her eyes. "No novel in the world could describe this," she said, taking in the toilet that flushed when you pulled a chain and a washtub so large it needed feet made to look like claws to prop it up off the floor. When Roselia turned the little spigot, the water rushed out the same as it did in Riley, but here in Fairmont, it warmed as it flowed, as if by magic, right in your own home. Imagine, Willa thought, turn the knob and there it is, hot water, cold water, whatever you want.

"Do you think . . ." Roselia hesitated. "Do you think we would have time to wash our hair before dinner?" Obviously she was still thinking about the silver hairbrush and how much she wanted to use it.

"If we hurry," Miss Grace said. "And before we go into town tonight I'll use my crimping irons to make it all curly if you like."

"Yes!" Roselia shouted, as if her black hair wasn't curly

all the time. But Willa couldn't wait. Maybe just being in such a wonderful house could make her beautiful too.

That night at dinner, Willa couldn't get over how much food there was: a large platter of fried chicken, a big bowl of coleslaw, three different vegetables so hot she could see the steam rise in thin white plumes above them. At each plate was a small dish of cut fresh fruit topped with sweet whipped cream. Crusty bread—yeast bread, not corn bread or sourdough—sat in a basket covered with a linen napkin.

"When are the other guests coming?" she asked, when Miss Grace passed the bread around a second time. The first roll had been so soft it had practically melted in Willa's mouth, but she didn't want to be greedy if there were others who had yet to eat.

"Other guests?" asked Mrs. McCartney, sitting across the table from them. She looked a lot like Miss Grace, only older. She wore pearls just like the doctor's wife had back in Riley. "Are we expecting anyone else?" she asked her daughter with a sigh, as if there were hordes of people coming and it was all Miss Grace's doing.

"Not that I know of," Miss Grace said, pushing her chicken around on her plate. She too had dressed for dinner, in a pale green dress that didn't look at all like the sensible blue skirt and white blouse Willa knew so well. Her friend looked glamorous, but not like her missionary self.

"You mean all this is just for us?" Willa asked. She couldn't believe it; there was no way the four of them could eat everything.

"Mr. McCartney will eat when he gets in later tonight, but his work at the bank will keep him later than usual." Although her voice was pleasant and she smiled, there was just something about Mrs. McCartney that made Willa nervous; it's like she keeps remembering our feet are bare, Willa thought, and she doesn't like that at the table. Thinking this made Willa angry—her shoes pinched so much that Miss Grace had insisted she not wear them to dinner—and also ashamed that she should think so badly of an older woman who had invited them to this home.

Roselia didn't say a word the entire meal. But the food on her plate disappeared; so did Willa's.

Willa couldn't help wondering about why people like the McCartneys had so much when so many others had so little. Not only food, but everything. Bright candles marched down the table, even though there were electric lights overhead, not to mention plenty of sunlight streaming through the many windows. Willa tried to make sense of the differences, but couldn't. She knew her family was eating soup beans again tonight while she sat down to a feast.

Perhaps Miss Grace realized how uncomfortable the two girls were, because they soon left the house and headed for town. The three of them walked the streets of Fairmont, peering into store windows and watching the many other people milling around. The streets were paved in blacktop and car after car, more than Willa had ever seen at any one time, whizzed up and down the avenue; horns blared and people called out to friends. Far over their heads the dome of the county courthouse became a great curved shadow as the sun set.

Downtown Fairmont was like the McCartney house: everything clean and bright. People laughed and talked, holding hands as they walked. Willa could see a theater up ahead, lights flashing. "Isn't the Depression here?" Willa asked Miss Grace as they walked.

Miss Grace paused and looked around. "Yes, it is. Even here in Fairmont, although on a Friday night it might be hard to tell."

"I'm glad it's not Depression," Roselia said, turning her head back and forth to catch everything. "I'm sick to death of the Depression."

"There are lots of parts of Fairmont that are hard hit. The mines nearby haven't been working for quite a while, just like over at Riley." She looked at Willa. "But right now, I just want you to have a very nice time."

"I intend to do just that," Roselia announced. She

twirled around, almost running into a man walking down the sidewalk.

"Pardon me, Miss," he said. Roselia's face turned so red that in the fading light she looked almost purple.

"Is that you, Grace?" asked a woman next to the strange man.

"Ginny!" Miss Grace said. Willa stepped back. This had already happened twice tonight—Miss Grace running into someone she knew and stopping to say hello.

But this was obviously someone special; Miss Grace reached out and hugged the woman. When they stepped back, Willa stared at the woman named Ginny, thinking that she was the most beautiful person she'd ever seen— even more beautiful than Miss Grace. Maybe it wasn't just the McCartney house but all of Fairmont that turned ugly ducklings into swans. Willa patted her own curly hair.

"Girls," Miss Grace said, turning to them. "This is my friend Ginny Kuhn. We went to school together."

"And who might you two be?" the woman asked. Her blue eyes turned up at the corners when she smiled just like Seraphina's did; Willa felt a wave of homesickness roll over her.

"This is Willa Lowell, and Roselia Olivetti. They are visiting with me from over at Riley Mines."

For a moment, Ginny's dancing eyes grew serious. "I heard you were working over there. How is it going?"

"I couldn't ask for two nicer friends than Willa and Roselia," Miss Grace said, and there was no hiding the real pride in her voice.

"Wayne and I were just on our way to get some ice cream at the drugstore," Ginny said. "It would be real nice if you would come with us." She sounded as though she really meant it, and Willa hoped that Miss Grace would say yes. Maybe it was the eyes, but she felt comfortable with this woman in a way she never could with Mrs. McCartney.

"Are you sure Wayne won't mind?" Miss Grace looked at the man who stood there, looking bemused.

"He won't mind in the least," Ginny insisted, as if he couldn't speak for himself. "Do you, doll? The more the merrier."

Willa wasn't so sure. The way he looked at his Ginny, there didn't seem room enough to see anyone else. With a catch of her breath, Willa remembered the look Daddy had given Mama, before he and Ves left for Hawk's Nest. Just seeing it made her ache a bit; feel a little hollow inside.

But she was the only one who had any doubts. "What do you say, girls?" Miss Grace asked. "Do you think you're up to some ice cream?"

"I am!" Roselia answered, obviously not embarrassed any longer.

Willa nodded. After that huge supper, Willa figured

she would never need to eat again, but ice cream sounded too good to pass up. Besides, she wanted to watch this Wayne; no one paid her any mind when she kept pace a few steps behind them—the sidewalks were too narrow for five people, after all. She noticed how he tucked Ginny's arm in his, and walked so closely, the sides of their bodies touching, as they made their way down the sidewalk. Once he leaned over and whispered something in her ear, making her hair move with his breath. Ginny laughed and bent her face so it rubbed against his shoulder, just a beat of a second.

Maybe, Willa hoped, someday a man will be like that with me. The idea made her sway a little, as though the warm evening air had rushed right through her and swirled about inside. A funny churning, a mixed-up sensation as though she'd been spinning around and suddenly stopped, but Willa found that she liked this feeling very much.

Chapter Ten

The next morning after breakfast (another meal with more food than could possibly be eaten) the three of them headed to visit Willa's Aunt Margaret. "She lives on Auberley Street. I have the number here," she told Miss Grace as they drove along in the little Studebaker coupé. Willa delighted in the car; Miss Grace had to squeeze this black, onion-shaped bulb to turn it on. The car hummed along, and the houses along Country Club Road flew by.

"That's over on the East Side," Miss Grace said. She made a left turn and headed back toward the town. "It won't take us more than a few minutes, though."

Under the glare of the morning sun, Willa began to see signs of the Depression that hadn't been noticeable the night before in the dimmer, cooler light. The streets no longer looked smooth, but were rutted with holes, rough with crumbled grit of rock and tar. The downtown didn't look quite so enticing; Willa saw the drugstore, its windows dusty now, and the theater. With the lights out, the gaps where a bulb had fallen out and not been replaced were all too obvious, like a missing tooth in a smiling mouth. There was none of the magic that had permeated the air the night before.

They crossed the big stone bridge to the East Side, where the roads grew smaller and even more winding on this side of the river. As they began looking for Aunt Margaret's street, the neighborhoods grew shabbier, with ramshackle houses fronted by tiny yards. Sometimes an old truck or rusted car was parked in front. Front windows had been boarded up just like back at Riley.

Secretly, Willa had been hoping that Aunt Margaret's house would be like the McCartneys'—a place she could be proud to claim, even if it was just kinship. But while it wasn't at all like that gracious place, she found herself liking Aunt Margaret's house for other reasons. Tall and thin, it looked surprisingly like a human face. The steeply gabled roof made a pointed hat, and the two windows had blinds pulled over them like sleeping eyes. But the porch was what made it funny; worn and stooped on either end, the once-white paint peeling in long strips, it looked for all the world like a great droopy mustache.

Built against a steep hill, the houses on Auberley Street had no front yards, only long rows of steps that rose in a sharp angle right off the road. Willa had often complained about running up and down the hill back in Riley, but she wasn't sure these steps were any better. The handrail wobbled beneath Willa's hand and she became dizzy when she looked behind her. When she reached the front porch, two pots of red geraniums sat on either side of the door.

"It's the mouth," Willa said, giggling.

"What's that?" Miss Grace asked, leaning forward to knock on the door.

Roselia shook her head in mock dismay at her friend's silliness. "Probably something she read in one of those books of yours."

Willa was about to explain when she heard a sound inside. They all three stared at the door, but no one answered.

"Maybe they didn't hear us," Miss Grace said, and knocked again. After a minute a little boy, maybe eight or nine years old, opened the door. Willa thought he looked a little like her brother Kyle.

"I'm looking for Margaret Anders," Miss Grace said. She gave the little boy a smile. He did not smile back.

The door opened wider, and a woman stood behind the boy. "Can I help you?" the woman asked. "I'm Margaret Anders." So this was the Aunt Margaret of Mama's stories! The woman who had once woken before dawn to steal Mama's only dress so she would have something new to wear to school! With nothing decent to wear herself, Mama had to stay home all day and sew.

"I'm Grace McCartney, a missionary over at Riley Mines . . ."

Willa heard the woman give a small cry, as though something had hurt her. At the sound, the doorway filled with people crowding about her aunt, who had put a hand to her mouth. "Well, come in and tell me what happened. There's always room for more, especially Esther's girls."

Miss Grace held up her hands. "You misunderstand, Mrs. Anders. Your niece, Willa Lowell, is visiting me from Riley. Her mother wanted her to meet you and deliver a letter. And this is her friend, Roselia Olivetti."

For the first time, Aunt Margaret seemed to really *see* Willa. And now that the crisis had passed, she lowered her hand, showing a happy smile. *Now* she looked like Mama and Willa found herself grinning back. "Come meet your cousin, everyone," she called to those behind her and held open the door. "Come in, come in!"

Willa stared into a dozen pair of eyes that stared right back. Everyone in the room looked like her, or someone in her family. The little boy that had greeted them did a somersault on the floor, just the way Kyle did, and the new baby sleeping in the dresser drawer buttoned his eyes up when he slept, same as Rusty. Although these were strangers to her, Willa felt exactly right.

"Let me introduce the crowd," Aunt Margaret said. "Most of these shysters are your Uncle Cecil's kids, who are boarding with us this summer." With great affection in her voice, she rattled off the list of names fast, as though Willa already knew them and only needed reminding as to who was whom. "Now the baby's mine—your cousin Emma. Named her after your grandmother, you know."

Willa hadn't. So Granny Kerns's name was Emma . . .

More people came into the room in addition to the cousins—sisters of Aunt Margaret's husband, each with a baby on her hip. And there was Uncle John, Mama's youngest brother, who was at work just now, but wouldn't he be disappointed to have missed Willa!

Noise, noise, noise; but despite the commotion, Willa enjoyed herself. She had not realized how quiet the McCartney household was until she came here.

"How's your mama doing?" Aunt Margaret asked.

"She's fine," she answered, unsure of what to say or how much to tell.

Aunt Margaret threw back her head and laughed; she sounded so much like Mama that Willa knew that if she just closed her eyes she could imagine she was back home in the coal camp.

"That's just what Esther herself would say; she's so prim and proper. Why, that girl could be dying and telling people that everything was fine. When your mama was a little girl she used to insist that we all sit down and play tea. 'Play tea,' I'd say! 'Who wants to play tea?' And when she married your daddy, she went out and bought flowers for all of us to wear during the wedding. Fanciest things I ever saw, those flowers. Cost her a fortune, but she always was one for wanting things nice." Aunt Margaret shook her head. "Did you know she wore a silk blouse when she got married?"

"No," Willa breathed.

Aunt Margaret nodded. "She spent a summer sewing alterations over in Fairmont for a store called The Bee Hive. They let her have it for cost and she was some proud of it, let me tell you."

"What happened to it?" Willa asked. Her mama? A silk blouse?

"You know, I couldn't say. When I saw her after you was born, I noticed she'd put on weight, you know how women do." Aunt Margaret lifted both hands and held them, fingers splayed, and waved them over her breasts. All the women in the room laughed.

Evidently Mama wasn't the only one in the family with a gift for mimicry, Willa thought.

"But I can't imagine she'd have thrown it out," Willa said, still trying to put the idea of her mother with something as expensive as a silk blouse. The idea of Mama being heavy was a surprise, too—while Mama's breasts were still round, there had been too many hard years of hunger to leave her with anything other than a thin, almost skinny frame. "I know I've never seen it."

"You'll have to ask her about it when you get home. And speaking of home, how's your daddy?" Her aunt put her hand to her chest and looked up. "I would have married him myself if Esther hadn't snapped him up. 'Course I was only a kid at the time. He still good looking?"

"Yes," Willa answered before thinking.

"That baby of his . . . what was his name?"

"You mean Ves?" Willa asked. (Imagine thinking of Ves as a baby!)

"That's right, Ves. He was a darling." Willa figured out that she wouldn't have to say much—her aunt would talk enough for the both of them. A dramatic storyteller, Aunt Margaret told Willa news about the family and plenty of tales concerning people Willa had never heard of; she tried to remember so she could repeat them later to Mama. For the first time, she learned that she had a great-aunt Willa and a great-great-aunt Laura too. "So I'm named for them," Willa said.

"Oh my, yes," Aunt Margaret said. "Esther always was one for naming people after someone else."

"Is there a Seraphina?"

"I think she had a teacher by that name."

"Kyle? Russell?"

"Kyle was your granddad's name, but I can't say about the Russell. Maybe he's one of your daddy's people."

So her grandparents were named Emma and Kyle. Willa remembered the talk she and Mama had had, about babies being part of a family. Every name was part of that and, surrounded by her relatives, Willa glimpsed what Mama had meant about bringing her old world to the Lowell cabin.

As they were leaving, Roselia whispered to Willa, "You have an awful nice family." Willa felt very proud. "All my family is back in Italy," Roselia said. "I've never met most of them." Willa put her arm around her friend's thin shoulders. She was used to envying Roselia—her pretty hair, her quick mind and confidence—but it was nice to be envied too.

All the way back to town, the two girls couldn't stop talking about Willa's family. "Your cousin Oliver is sooooo cute," Roselia said, her dark eyes blinking furiously, as though he could see her bat them at him, never mind that he was now miles away. "But not as handsome as your brother."

"My brother?" Willa asked. "You mean Kyle?"

Roselia blushed. "No, I mean Ves."

Willa could not believe this. She had never thought of Ves as handsome, or anything else other than Ves. As far as she knew, Ves didn't have a special girlfriend, but he had been away so long, anything might be possible. She wondered if Ves had ever looked at a girl the way Mr. Wayne had looked at Miss Ginny last night. Not that he would have told Willa. If a boy ever looked at her like that, Willa wouldn't want to tell another soul but would keep it special to herself.

Instead of returning to the McCartney house, they pulled up in front of a church with huge pillars rising up in the front. It was bigger even than the company store back home. Willa felt small, standing in its shadow.

"I have a surprise for you," Miss Grace said, climbing out of the car. "Let's go around the back and I'll show you." She sounded excited and held up a key ring as though about to open a treasure chest. Willa and Roselia followed her to the back of the building and through a narrow door.

In a room so large it echoed when they spoke, Miss Grace pulled out some large boxes. "These are all the clothes families have donated. Some are hardly worn at all, and I was thinking I might be able to find you some new dresses."

Roselia gave a small squeal and grabbed Willa's hand. Willa held her breath, hardly knowing what to say. She had her old dress, back in Riley, and the new blouse and skirt Mama had made over for her to wear to Fairmont. If she found another dress here that would be more clothes than Willa had ever owned at one time in her whole life.

Together, the girls peered into the boxes, lifting out dress after dress and holding them up against their bodies. Each seemed better than the last, but Willa was particularly taken by one Miss Grace held up: pink with white polka dots, it even had the white middy tie she'd dreamed about. When Miss Grace handed it to Roselia and suggested she try it on, Willa could hardly keep from pleading that she wanted it too.

"This is a marvelous color for you," Miss Grace said to Roselia. She pointed to a screen in the corner of the room. "You can change over there."

Roselia took the dress and vanished.

"Let's see what's here for you, Willa." Miss Grace reached into the trunk. The next dress was cream colored with red trim. Willa found it very pretty, but Miss Grace was already putting it aside. "Perhaps your mama might like this," she said, folding it neatly.

The next dress, dark blue with flowers all over it, was much too small. "Perhaps Seraphina . . ." It joined the cream-colored one. Willa began to worry that there was a dress in the box for everyone but her.

Three more were much too long, and one, made of black satin, smelled so badly of sweat and old perfume that Miss Grace threw it over in the corner. "Evidently, it is too much to ask *some* people to wash a dress before they give it away," she muttered. Willa couldn't help but glance over at it. The satin had been awfully elegant.

"Here we go," Miss Grace said, reaching in the box. She pulled up a gray-and-white-striped dress with a black velvet collar. The front wasn't a middy style at all, but looked more like a soldier's uniform, curlicued with black braid. "This looks like just the thing."

Willa took the dress and held it against her. It was all right, but not as pretty as Roselia's.

Just then her friend came out from behind the screen, a swirl of pink and white. "How do I look?" she asked, her voice rising like a song. She danced with an imaginary partner across the room.

Miss Grace nodded and looked pleased. "You can see yourself in the mirror over there," she said. "What do you think, Willa?"

"It's gorgeous," Willa told her friend. But the bright color of Roselia's dress only made Willa's gray one seem all the more drab and ordinary.

Just then, a flash of red caught her eye. Dropping the gray dress, Willa picked it up—yes! This was the one! It looked just like the dress Tori wore the night Rusty had been born. "Can I try this one on?" she asked.

Miss Grace frowned a little. "If you think it will fit."

Willa dashed behind the screen.

The buttons went up the side, and Willa was so excited that her fingers fumbled trying to fasten them. When she'd finished, she noticed there were some gaps where the fabric pulled too tight, but if she kept her arms at her sides, no one would be able to see. She twirled a little. The skirt didn't billow beneath her knees, but the length was all right. Lots of women wore dresses this short—in Fairmont, anyway. Willa pictured herself going back to Riley and explaining that her dress was actually the latest fashion.

But when she stepped out from behind the screen, Willa could tell by her friends' faces that the dress was all wrong. Still, she couldn't let it go. "It fits fine," she said. "Real fine."

Miss Grace looked at Willa for a long time, and then glanced at the gray dress Willa had tossed to the side. "If you think so, Willa," was all she said. "I do agree that you look nice in the red."

She could have the red dress! Willa reached up and began to twirl like Roselia had done. She lifted her arms high. Under her arm, fabric began to tear—the ripping sound so loud that it seemed to fill the whole room. When one of the buttons popped off, Willa felt her cheeks grow hot and she ran behind the screen.

"It's all right," Miss Grace called to her. But it wasn't. Blinking back hot tears, Willa took off the dress and held it up so she could see it. Seraphina would someday be just the right size—if not next year, then perhaps the one following. Mama could fix the tear and sew the button back on. She wiped her eyes with the backs of her hands and put her old clothes back on. Chin held high, she stepped back out into the room.

"I guess," Willa said, trying not to see how disappointed both Miss Grace and Roselia seemed—Roselia looked almost in tears herself. "I don't think the red dress fits after all. But Seraphina might look mighty nice in red, so maybe she could have it."

"Of course she can, Willa," Miss Grace said in a gentle voice. She held up the other dress. "And I know the gray dress isn't as pretty as the red, but would you like to try it on?" Willa nodded, afraid that if she said any more all the feelings she had inside of her might break her in two. Taking the dress, she went back behind the screen.

When she came out and saw herself in the mirror, she was surprised how smart she looked. The black velvet collar made her white throat look longer and the black braiding swelled over her chest. For the first time in her life, Willa decided that maybe she looked a little like Mama. Roselia, in her middy dress, looked pretty, but still like Roselia. Willa's skirt was fuller and longer than Roselia's too. This was a grown-up dress.

"You know," she said to Miss Grace, still looking in the mirror. "I think, after all, that this is the right dress for me."

Chapter Eleven

B ack in Riley Mines, every piece of new clothing was held up and admired.

"Your father is going to love this sweater," Mama said, smoothing the soft brown wool. "He'll look quite the gentleman in it."

"I tried to get Daddy work clothes," Willa explained. After all, Daddy wasn't one of the coal operators who sat in an office all day. Deep inside the mine, the hot temperatures could make wearing wool very uncomfortable. Then there were days when Daddy would work in a shaft filled with water sometimes a foot or more deep, kneeling in a liquid so heavy with minerals and acid it ate its way through the strongest fabrics. Wool would soon feel twice as heavy. "Miss Grace said that people donate what they have, and in Fairmont they don't get many work clothes or overalls—things like that."

Mama tipped her head to the side and studied the sweater. "I'm just as glad to have something so fancy," she said. "I can't remember the last time your daddy bought himself anything other than overalls. Seeing him in a sweater will take us back to when we were courting."

Speaking of courting reminded Willa about Mama's silk blouse. But before she could ask about it, Seraphina burst into the room. "Look at me!" She danced around in the red dress, bumping into the stove long enough (Willa grimaced) to streak a black line of soot across the back of the skirt. "Ain't I grown up?"

Willa and Mama looked at each other, and then burst out laughing.

"What?" Sera demanded, her pretty face bewildered.

"The dress is very nice," Mama was quick to say, trying to control her twitching mouth without success.

"You look like you've been trying on Mama's clothes," Willa said at the same time. Back in Fairmont, the dress had nearly burst over Willa's body, but here in Riley, it hung on the ten-year-old's smaller one. The shoulder seams sagged nearly two inches longer than her bony frame and the skirt almost touched the ground. "It will be filthy in ten minutes. Why not wear the blue dress I brought you and wait to grow into this one?" Willa couldn't help but be a bit sorry she'd brought it home.

"The blue dress would fit you better," Mama agreed. "And the color suits you."

Sera scowled and folded her arms across her chest. "I like this one." She gritted her teeth together just like Ves did when he was angry. "When can I go and show Theresa?" she asked. "You said she got a new dress too."

"Soon," Willa said. The trip to Fairmont had only been overnight, but there was so much to catch up on. "Did you get a letter while I was gone?"

Mama shook her head. "Maybe tomorrow." She didn't sound worried, but Willa could see the V-shaped frown between her eyes. "Come here and let me roll up your sleeves, Sera."

"We'll probably get two letters together," Willa said, matching Mama's casual tone. "You remember when that happened back in May?"

"That's likely," Mama agreed. She gathered up the clothes and the secondhand shoes Miss Grace had helped Willa buy in Fairmont. Mama had given her a few of the precious dollars to get them, along with tracings of Seraphina and Kyle's feet to match to the best size possible. "Get them a tad big," Mama had advised. "Not so that you'll trip in them, but they're for fall, not right now, and feet will grow." Willa loved trying on shoes to get just the right fit. After experimenting with four pairs, she finally narrowed it down to two: leather oxfords that looked ordinary and sturdy enough, and a pair of sharp black boots with little heels. Willa had bought the boots, and was pretty sure what Mama would say, but that would take care of itself when the time came. All the shoes were put away until the cold weather set in.

"Help me store these lovely winter things and then you two can scoot down to the Olivettis' and admire all their prizes as well," Mama told them.

Willa wrinkled her nose as she picked up the package of mothballs Miss Grace had included. "The whole room is going to smell," she said, glad that she wouldn't have to sleep in here. This was where Ves and Kyle usually slept, if Ves had been home, but Mama and the little boys had been here all summer, leaving the big room empty at night.

"Beats opening the box and finding nothing but a few holes," Mama said. "No, Kyle," she said, taking them from the little boy who had gathered a few and was rolling them like marbles. "Willa, would you get your brother's trucks before you go?" The trucks were only pieces of square wood, so crusted from use that Willa hated to touch them. Her brother wasn't happy to have the new toy taken away, and stomped outside.

Seraphina and Willa were almost out the door before Willa remembered to ask, "Aunt Margaret said you wore a silk blouse when you got married. What ever happened to it?"

Mama, who had been reaching to pick Rusty up, stopped suddenly. "Why do you ask?"

Her mother's distant, formal tone flustered Willa. "I don't know . . . well, it's just that silk is so expensive . . . ," she said, fumbling over the words. Mama didn't look at her, but at a spot somewhere by the stove. "I mean, not even the coal operators' wives own silk blouses. And it was fun to think we might have one."

"Well, we don't," Mama said—almost snapped. "Not for a long time."

"What's silk?" Seraphina asked.

Unsure just what was going on, Willa tried to answer as calmly as she could. "It's a type of cloth." There was a bolt of it—sky blue—in the company store, but Willa didn't know if Seraphina had even seen it; Willa didn't think it had ever been taken from the shelf. "I've heard"—although Willa couldn't remember who could have told her this— "that it feels like a spider's web."

Seraphina's lip curled. "That doesn't sound nice at all."

Mama's whole body jerked. Her grip on Rusty was so tight the baby squirmed. "It feels," she said slowly, "like putting your hand in a barrel of soft rain water—like a second skin. That blouse was the most beautiful thing I've ever owned."

"What happened to it?" Seraphina asked.

To Willa's horror, Mama began to cry—not great gulping sobs the way Willa shed them, in a burst of light and heat, but heavy tears that ran down her cheeks without any sound at all. "A few years ago, before you were born, between you and Willa, actually, I had a baby."

Willa knew what was coming. She wished she could grab Sera by the hand and haul her out of the cabin rather than watch her mother's pain.

"We named him Earl—after your daddy's father. Not that he lived very long. The doctor said there was something wrong with his mouth. He couldn't suck. He wouldn't eat." Mama bent her head to Rusty's and brushed her cheek against his hair.

"He cried about three days straight before he died." Mama's gaze wandered to a point above their heads. "I used my blouse to wrap him in when we buried him."

This was the last thing Willa wanted to hear after such a happy time in Fairmont. She'd wanted everyone to be delighted with the presents—and they were—but if only there was a way to go back a few minutes in time; to walk out of the cabin for a visit with Roselia and Theresa; to never have asked about the silk at all.

To Willa's surprise, Seraphina went over and hugged her mother. "I wish I'd known I had another brother," she said. "You should have told me."

"You're right," Mama said, bending down and giving

Sera a kiss on the top of her head. And then, seeing Willa standing there, Mama came over and kissed her too.

Down at the Olivettis', Roselia's father was just getting home from the harvest truck. He looked tired but pleased as he emptied a sack filled with produce. They all stared at the food: corn still in its husks; green peppers so shiny they looked unreal; tomatoes, a little bruised, but red and juicy still; cucumbers and early squash, all tumbled together on the small table.

"We'll eat well tonight," he told his wife, taking her in his arms and kissing her firmly on the mouth.

"Indeed we will," Mrs. Olivetti told him, throwing her arms around him and kissing him right back. They were so different from Mama and Daddy—Mama's kisses this afternoon aside. The whole Olivetti family was affectionate in a way the Lowells never could be; Roselia and Theresa never left the house without Mrs. Olivetti telling them she loved them and kissing them on both cheeks as though she might never see them again. "Mama," Roselia would complain, rolling her eyes, but Willa thought it was nice.

But today, Willa only had eyes for the food. Last year Ves and Daddy worked with Mr. Olivetti, rising before the sun was up to go in trucks to farms where their labor was paid in food. Every night they brought home their spoils and Willa and Mama would can in the hot steaming kitchen for winter supplies. This year, Willa realized, there would be nothing to can unless she went and picked herself.

"Can I go and help too?" she asked Mr. Olivetti.

"What?" The man laughed and plucked her cheek. "You think that God made girls to stand out in the fields doing a man's work?"

"No," Willa said, although this was exactly what she thought—after all, Mama grew up on a farm and talked plenty about bringing the harvest in by any means necessary. "I was just asking." The husks around the corn looked papery. Willa longed to touch them.

Mr. Olivetti grew serious. "There aren't many men who are going to appreciate a girl working; not if it means a man might not be able to provide for his family." He spoke gently, and Willa knew he was thinking that Daddy and Ves were far away. "Perhaps," he said and glanced over at his wife. "Perhaps we could find something here to share?"

Mrs. Olivetti hesitated. Only the briefest, barest moment, and then she was offering, even insisting. But the pulse of worry about not having enough had not been lost on Willa. "I don't want anything I can earn for myself," she insisted.

"You can't earn," Mr. Olivetti told her. "You do understand, don't you?"

"Yes," Willa replied, but only to be polite. She didn't understand at all. If a family needed food and she was strong enough to earn it, why couldn't she get on the truck like the men and older boys did?

"We ought to be going," she said. And the Olivettis didn't hold them back. Not even Roselia and Theresa; there was a big supper to prepare, and fresh food to enjoy. Willa cared too much about the Olivettis to deny them this rare pleasure, no matter how much she longed for some of the produce herself.

Once outside, Willa told Seraphina to head on home and she'd be there in a minute. "You gonna go see Miss Grace?" Sera asked. This was such a common event in the Lowell family that she dashed off without waiting for an answer.

Willa walked down the road. Somehow she would find a way to get on the truck in the morning. The first thing she needed to know was what time it came.

Over by the company store, some boys and young men were hanging about. Willa could see from their dusty clothes—brown dirty dust, not black soot—that they'd been picking that day with Mr. Olivetti. When they saw her coming, they stopped talking and stared at her; she could hear the chewing tobacco flying fast and furious, and Willa hoped that none of it would get on her dress. Men chewed, Ves had explained once, to keep the grit from settling in their teeth and drying out their mouths down in the mines. Daddy had once been a chewer, but like his courting sweaters, tobacco was one of the many things he gave up as times grew harder.

"Can any of you tell me what time the harvest trucks pull out of here?" Willa asked, hoping her voice wasn't as high pitched and girlish as she feared. There wasn't another woman anywhere to be found on the steps.

"Who wants to know?" a boy asked—someone not much older than Seraphina by the looks of him. Willa glared. She wasn't afraid of the likes of him!

"I'm just asking."

"And I ain't telling," the boy answered with a laugh. Some of the others joined in as though he'd said something very witty.

But they stopped when one of the older boys—a young man, really, tall and big as Ves, rose and walked over to her. He stood on the steps and looked down, and Willa could see a small crescent-shaped scar on his cheek that made him look fierce and the almost downy pencil line of a mustache over his lip that made him look as though he hadn't finished growing yet. She preferred staring at the mustache.

"Why do you want to know?" he asked. His eyes went over her, from the top of her head all the way down to her bare toes. "You don't look like any boy I ever saw."

"I'm just asking," Willa repeated. She didn't know if she liked him staring at her or not. A flutter went through her, as though a bird had taken up residence deep inside. Trying to keep some pride, she made it a point to raise her chin. "Don't bother," she told him, and spun around so quickly that her feet slipped in the dirt and she almost fell. Hearing the laughter behind her, Willa ran off.

She'd almost made it to her cabin when she heard someone calling her name. Not sure if she should, she turned around. It was the scar-faced one, only now, away from the crowd, he didn't look quite so strange. He was holding his hands out in front of him as though he expected her to charge at him.

"How do you know my name?" she demanded.

He caught up to her. "You're Ves's kid sister, ain't you? I'm Johnny Settle. He told me to keep an eye out on you while he was gone."

"Oh," Willa said. "I didn't recognize you." Growing up, she'd seen Johnny messing around with her brother, but the rough-and-tumble boy didn't seem the same person as the nearly grown man standing there with her.

Johnny smiled. "Took me a minute to realize who you was." Again, she could feel his eyes on her, his gaze almost like fingers. There was a stirring in her gut again, and Willa clasped her hands in front of her as if to hide all that was happening within her. "You've rather grown up yourself."

"It's probably the dress," Willa told him. He had a nice smile, she thought, no longer feeling humiliated, as she had back in town. "One of the ladies in Miss Grace's church donated it." She stepped back and smoothed the skirt.

Johnny's eyes hardened. "You ain't ashamed to wear charity goods?"

Fury raced through Willa. "I'm wearing a *dress*," she shot back.

"Still something no one wanted," Johnny taunted. "Bet it made them feel good, giving it away."

"People can feel what they like," Willa said, raising her chin. "And so can you. But when someone who has too much gives away something to another who has too little, I don't call that charity, I call that doing right." She was about to storm off when Johnny broke out laughing.

"Ves always said you were a Tartar," he told her, and there was no mistaking the admiration in his voice, filling the hole where the scorn had been.

Willa felt her face burn. The person who gave away the dress wasn't the only one who had helped her—if anyone had done right by the Lowells this summer, it was Johnny Settle. Every day, the coal box under the house was filled with the fuel they needed. Willa knew that Johnny risked being arrested or even beaten by the guards if he was caught in the mine, stealing the coal. "I guess I should thank you for helping us out this summer." Her voice could not have been less gracious.

Johnny didn't seem to mind. "That's between your

brother and me," he said, but he leaned closer toward her. The white scar was so close that Willa could have reached out and touched it. "I just hadn't realized that Ves's kid sister was so pretty."

That was the second time he'd said that—not that she was pretty, but the "kid" part. "I'm not so young," Willa said, her voice stiff but not quite so cold. What would the scar feel like? Was it smooth like a button or knobby like a knothole in a piece of wood? "Ves is just a year and a half ahead of me."

Johnny nodded. "I can see that."

As they stood there, Willa hoped that he'd say something more; that something brilliant and charming would come into her own head. But she seemed emptied of words, as if reading all the novels and poems in the world could never have prepared her for this moment.

"Mama will be looking for me," she told him at last.

"The truck leaves about four," he said. She must have looked puzzled because he added, "The one leaving for the harvest."

The harvest. The food. So that was why he'd come looking for her. And *I'll be on it,* Willa thought as she thanked him, then went inside. Mama looked up as she entered, and Willa wondered if she would see the bright cheeks and ask about what she'd been up to, but all she said was that supper was ready. The Olivetti table with its plentiful fresh food rose up like a ghost before Willa's eyes. If the truck comes at four, Willa planned, that gives me about ten hours to turn myself into a boy. She smiled a little sadly to herself and looked down at her dress; seemed a shame, considering how much she'd just enjoyed being a girl.

Chapter Twelve

After everyone else in the family had gone to bed, Willa, carrying a soft bundle, slipped out of the house and headed down for the Mission. The big picture window was dark, a heavy curtain pulled over the front of it. But upstairs, where Miss Grace lived, Willa could see a window in the back that was faintly lit.

The steps to the second floor ran up the outside of the building, and they creaked unsteadily as Willa ran up them. The third one wobbled, causing Willa to lose her balance; she fell with a thud against the door instead of knocking on it.

"Who's there?" Miss Grace called out through the closed door.

"It's me, Willa."

"Willa? What are you doing out this time of night?" The lock on the door snapped open and Miss Grace stood there wearing a cotton shift so plain it might have been Willa's own. "Is everything all right?"

"We're all fine," Willa said. "I just need some help and I didn't know where else to turn." She hoped that her friend wouldn't scold. There wasn't any time.

"Well, come in then." Miss Grace stepped back and let Willa through. Then she turned on some lamps. "Just give me a minute to change and I'll be back."

While she was gone, Willa looked around the room. Although she had been going to the Mission nearly every night for months, although she had visited with Miss Grace and her family in Fairmont, Willa had never had a reason to be here in Miss Grace's private apartment.

Now that she was here, Willa understood why. Or why Miss Grace preferred to spend her time downstairs in the Mission itself. The room was barren almost to the point of ugliness: no carpets, no curtains, no fancy chair other than a wooden one by a desk holding a Bible and some papers—letters, they appeared to be; the ink on one of them was not yet dry. Willa was about to open the Bible— she often heard Miss Grace quote from it, but had never read it—when her friend came back into the room dressed in her customary blue skirt and blouse.

"You look confused," Miss Grace said. She pulled the chair away from the desk and sat in it.

Willa glanced around the room. "It's so empty."

Miss Grace looked around, as though someone else lived here and she was seeing it for the first time. "Well, I don't spend a lot of time here—I'm mostly downstairs where I'm surrounded by plenty of creature comforts." She smiled ruefully. "My mother is hoping it's just a phase." Willa was about to ask what a "phase" was when Miss Grace reached for the pile of clothes Willa had brought: a pair of threadbare coveralls, a shirt, and a cap so faded that the black was now a military green. Miss Grace raised her eyebrows. "What are you up to now?"

"I need you to make me into a boy," Willa told her.

"A what?" Miss Grace almost shrieked.

"A boy." Willa picked up the coveralls and held them up against her, trying not to think that earlier today she'd enjoyed all those pretty dresses. "The harvest trucks are going out to farms, and they won't let a girl go, even if there is no man around in the family to go. But I *have* to go; it might not look like much, but we need that food to get us through the winter that's coming."

"I see." Miss Grace stood up and tapped her fingers over her mouth as though it was a musical instrument. "But Willa, there's no way . . ." She held her hands out and gestured. "Look at you. No one is going to mistake you for a boy."

"Not even if you cut my hair?" Willa asked.

"Cut . . . oh my." Miss Grace sat down again.

Willa grinned. "You remember back when we were talking about how novels didn't mean much to me? The night you read me poetry for the first time?" Miss Grace nodded. "Well, I've finally found something in *Little Women* that makes sense. I'm going to cut my hair like Jo did."

Miss Grace laughed so hard that her eyes watered. "Leave it to you to justify yourself through a book," she said when she had caught her breath. "What does your mother say about cutting your hair?"

"Well, you know Mama. She understands."

"So you haven't told her yet."

Willa brushed this aside; they were wasting time. "I just thought she'd understand better if she saw me all ready to go."

Seeing that Willa had made up her mind, Miss Grace went to get the scissors.

As she climbed in the truck the next morning, the men and older boys around her were too tired and sleepy to care whether she was a girl or not. Still, Willa couldn't help but take some satisfaction in the job they had done: the hair was gone—not as short as some, but there wasn't a tendril dangling coyly beneath the faded cap. On her hands—too small to go with a boy's lanky body—she wore a pair of old gardening gloves Miss Grace had found.

With needles, thread, and the now infamous scissors, the two of them had worked long into the night to make Ves's old coveralls and blue work shirt he'd grown out of last year into a big shapeless mass. Just when Willa was about to give up in despair because her breasts just would *not* stay hidden, Miss Grace ran downstairs and came back up with a medical kit filled with wound bandages. "Go in my room and wrap these bandages around yourself."

Once Willa was decked out as though she had been injured in a war, the breasts were gone. The bandages pinched and made it hard to breathe, but there was no denying they were effective.

But the final and most perfect disguise was simple dirt. Willa had smeared some over her face, covering her freckles and nose; making her chin squarer and her ears less noticeable. "Mama always told us that if we didn't keep our faces clean then the dirt was all anyone would see," Willa told Miss Grace. "Guess I'm about to see if she was right."

At dawn that same morning, Willa passed her first test. When Mama woke and saw her, she immediately said, "What on earth is that covering your face?" Then she noticed the rest of the clothes. "There had better be a good explanation for this, young lady."

When Willa was done explaining, Mama didn't look any happier, but she hurried to pack a lunch bucket and told Willa that she and Seraphina would get out the canning jars and get them ready. Seraphina glared at Willa, and Willa recalled how she had felt, being stuck in the house all day when it seemed Ves was the one who got to run free.

After only a few hours in the fields, Willa would have been happy enough to spend even a minute inside. Her cap kept the hot sun out of her eyes but by late morning the bare skin on the back of her neck which her hair had once covered had burned red. Some of the men wore handkerchiefs tied under their chins but others just let the burns gradually turn brown as the days went on.

The first weeks were the hardest. A string of sunny, summer days—thirteen of them in a row—prodded Willa to rise every day well before dawn and shrug into the strange, heavy clothes. The bandages reeked of sweat and grime, but Willa determinedly wrapped herself in them every morning. Then she ran down to the pump, bringing up plenty of water for the family to begin their day, only to gulp down some breakfast and run back into town as the truck was pulling in.

Farm work, done by hand, was hard and monotonous. Beans had to be picked in the morning, before the dew was off of them, so Willa and some of the younger boys found themselves bending over, not moving more than a few baby steps at a time. Every time she stood to stretch, it was only a reminder of how much longer the row was, looming before them. Sometimes, when they worked farms higher up the mountains, the rows were planted at an angle, and Willa soon learned to walk in a clip-clopped manner to keep her balance.

During dinnertime, after she had eaten a bite of cold bacon and biscuits, Willa would sometimes doze beneath the shade of a tree, sitting well away from the others. She didn't dare join in the conversations, for fear her voice would give her away. When she arrived home at night, Willa was too tired after her cold supper to do anything other than wash her face and tumble into bed. Days went by before she realized that she'd uttered only a few sentences to anyone.

But as the time passed, there were more and more cans of food. More than once, Willa ran her fingers over the glass jars, reading with her fingers the raised letters of the manufacturer's name. Her world had become one without spoken words at all.

After the second week, the pains in her muscles became a steady but tolerable ache and her hands—gloves or no gloves—were toughening up. Willa found that she wasn't as tired as she had once been, and began to enjoy her lunches. Mama sewed a pocket in the overalls, inside where no one could see it, and Willa sometimes sneaked in some reading time beneath the trees. Her poets did not disappoint her; indeed, they seemed to understand how short her time was and offered up their best.

Willa's favorite place to work was the cornfields, where the rows of towering plants hid her as effectively as any disguise. She could risk removing her cap or gloves to enjoy the coolness of a breeze blowing off the mountain. The tearing of the corn from the tall leafy plant created a fearsome noise (when she factored in the dozens of people who were making it around her), and Willa softly recited poems to herself as she worked; the snowy lines of a writer like Robert Frost (how appropriately named!) were a special challenge in the late July heat that sat upon the fields like a blanket.

One day, after such a morning, Willa pulled out an unexpected treat from her bucket—a swirl of molasses spread upon her biscuit. The syrupy sweetness cooled her tongue like a long drink of water. She cracked open a new book titled *Leaves of Grass* by a poet called Walt Whitman that Miss Grace had brought up just last night. As she read, Willa nibbled slowly to make the pleasure last. She had put the very last crumb in her mouth just as a shadow fell over her.

"I knew you'd find a way, Willa Lowell," the man said.

Willa stopped chewing. The food, which had been her delight just moments ago, sat heavy inside her stomach. Despite all of her efforts, even cutting her hair, she'd been caught. Well, they can't take away the food I've already earned, she told herself. I did that much, anyway.

But the man didn't make a fuss. In fact, he removed his own cap and sat down beside her. Out of the glare of the light, Willa gave a sigh of relief when she saw that it was Johnny Settle. In the few weeks since she'd seen him, his skin had darkened, making his black hair and downy mustache less noticeable. She could barely make out the bump of the scar.

"That day, over in Riley, when you kept pestering everyone about the trucks, I knew what you were trying to do." He grinned at her, as though she'd done something charming, when all she'd done was prove him right.

"You been watching me all this time?" she asked.

On the one hand, she didn't like knowing she'd been watched, but on the other hand, it was sort of nice, thinking that he'd noticed her. So she wasn't sure if she was disappointed or not when he said, "Naw, I've been going across the state line into Greene County. There's a man that hires a bunch of us every year. He doesn't go back and forth, though, so we bunk in his barn." Johnny gave a sigh. "He's got this great big pond, right in the middle of his northern field, complete with a wooden platform right in the middle. Swimming there is just heaven."

"Wish I could go somewhere like that," Willa said. "Seraphina swims on the sly, but I haven't gone since Daddy used to take us years ago. We'd shimmy down to our underwear . . ." Realizing what she'd just said, Willa turned beet red. She'd been talking as if he were one of her family, or Roselia. What would he think of her? And if Mama ever found out. . . . "I didn't mean . . . ," she started to say.

Johnny smiled. "You're a nice girl, Willa Lowell."

She had no idea what one was supposed to say to that. Yes, she was, which was true but sounded proud, or no, she wasn't, which might sound humble, but could lead him to think almost anything?

"How did you know it was me?" she asked. "Did I do it wrong, dress wrong, I mean?"

"Well, you look fine to me—I mean, you don't stand out. And I like your hair short—makes you look older somehow."

"Then how did you know?" She wasn't worried anymore—if he was going to turn her in, he would turn her in. After going for weeks without a real conversation, it was nice, sitting here and talking.

"No man I know sits and reads at dinnertime." Johnny pointed to the book she'd dropped on her lap when she'd noticed him. "What's it about?"

Willa glanced at him, trying to see if he was kidding her. "It's some poems," she told him, her voice cautious.

"You like to read?" He didn't sound teasing.

"More than anything," Willa told him. "I've been studying since Miss Grace came. I want to read every book in her library, but the poetry's my favorite." She thought he might say something snide about the Mission being about charity too, but he didn't.

Instead he seemed interested. "So read me something."

"What?"

"A poem, I guess; if that's what you got." He leaned back against a poplar tree. When she didn't say anything, he asked, "Well?"

"Nothing," Willa said hastily, and flipped open the book:

Song of Myself

I celebrate myself, and sing myself
And what I assume you shall assume,
For every atom belonging to me as
    good belongs to you.

Now what would he think of that, she wondered. But his eyes were still closed, so Willa kept reading:

I loafe and invite my soul,
I lean and loafe at my ease observing
    a spear of summer grass.

My tongue, every atom of my blood,
    form'd from this soil, this air,

Born here of parents born here
from parents the same, and their
parents the same . . .

For more than five minutes she read, her voice trembling at first as she read about "light kisses, a few embraces, a reaching around of arms." Johnny had opened his eyes and was watching her—she could feel his eyes upon her as though she were staring back at him—but he never moved until the foreman blew the whistle calling them back to work.

"What does it all mean?" Johnny asked, as they walked back.

"I don't know." Willa tried to keep her voice low—it was all well and good that Johnny knew who she was, but there was no reason to be careless. She shoved the book deep down inside her coveralls and pulled on her gloves; she covered her head with her cap.

He must not have heard her because he asked again. They were standing near the foreman, who was making afternoon assignments. Willa shook her head. "What?" he whispered.

"My voice will give me away," she hissed, directly into his ear. She was so close to him that she could smell the dusty heat of his hair; his ears were clean and a little paler on top, where an inch of hair fell over them.

"Hey, boss," Johnny called out, startling her so that she jumped. "How about letting me and my friend work in the tomato patch today? Noticed they need weeding."

"Do what you want," the man growled. And Willa soon found herself working well away from the others. As they knelt in the dirt and pulled the weeds, they talked about the poem.

"There was a lot of words about the earth in it," Johnny said. "Seems like the man who wrote it knows something about working. Not at all what I would think a book person might know."

"It's certainly earthy enough," Willa muttered, wondering how she'd dared to read it to him at all, and was pleased when Johnny laughed.

"I liked it," he told her. "You know any others?"

"Yes," Willa answered.

"Tell me."

She did.

From then on, Johnny often worked side by side with her, either in the next row or just across the way. If they weren't close or alone enough to talk, she could always count on looking up and meeting his eyes, smiling when she noticed him. As a young man well-known and admired in the group, he had no qualms about asking for a choice assignment or a place where they might be alone. At first Willa figured that he was asking to learn more about poetry, for he seemed to enjoy it. Soon he was committing lines to memory, and would chuckle when Willa would stutter over lines like "My darling, my darling, my life and my bride" (Who knew that even Edgar Allan Poe would prattle on so much about love?) as he said them back to her.

Sometimes he would quote a line out of context or with the words mixed up—he had a playful quality about him that Willa was learning to like. There were moments where he could be, well, such a *boy*, and he wasn't above teasing her by tossing a few corn kernels at her if he decided that she wasn't paying him enough attention, or dropping some cold wet stones down her back to make her gasp.

But the time he reached out and brushed the back of her head with a long blade of grass, making her think at first that the gnats were swarming; when she spun around and stood so close to him that she could feel his breath on her face; when they shared "light kisses, a few embraces, a reaching around of arms," well, none of that seemed very silly at all.

Chapter Thirteen

From her front porch, Willa stared out at the rain. This was the third day of foul weather; yesterday marble-sized hail had pelted Riley Mines, chattering against the roof and windows of the Lowell cabin like teeth. There would be no harvest work again today, and it was too wet and miserable for Willa to think about running off to meet Johnny up at the pioneer cabin.

Together, they had made the square of foundation stones a special place; a world where no one existed except the two of them. When they lay side by side in the grass, their hands clasped, looking up at the stars, it was easy to imagine that they were somewhere else, even other people. Willa had come to feel this way whenever Johnny was about—as though she had stepped out of her faded, worn-out self and into a shiny new one. Johnny told her she was beautiful. Sometimes they would pretend they were pioneers and this was to be their new home. He told her that he loved her. They talked less about books now, and they kissed more, but just thinking about the kissing made Willa feel all hot and shivery inside, as vivid as dreams before waking.

"What's that coming along the road?" Mama asked. She was sitting next to Willa, her sewing in her hands, but she hadn't bothered to thread a needle yet. The rain made them all sleepy and languid, as though their bones had melted around the edges.

"I don't see anything," Willa answered, not even bothering to look; she wished she could be with Johnny. For the first time, home seemed a little dull. "When's this rain supposed to stop? I'm going to go soft, with all this sitting around," she grumbled.

"I doubt that," Mama said. "What about you bring out that book Miss Grace brought you the other day—the one about the boy who goes down the river on a raft."

Willa sighed and sprawled as though she would never be comfortable again. "Didn't sound like something that would interest me." Caught up in her own boredom she didn't see the look that Mama gave her.

Down in the town, a truck pulled up at the company store and some men got out. "There is someone down there—now who would be fool enough to travel on such a horrid day?" Mama leaned forward to see better.

With some effort, Willa peered down too. The truck wasn't one she recognized—not that she expected anyone to come asking for workers, but you never knew. Some farmers pushed too hard; they'd heard about a boy over in Preston County, killed when lightning struck the hoe he'd been carrying. He'd been dead, people said, before he'd hit the ground, his hair burned off his head.

She and Johnny got caught in a rainstorm once. Nothing like this ceaseless drumming, but a lovely summer shower that made their hair cling to their heads like winter caps; water droplets trickling like wine (the poets were always comparing things to wine) making their kisses all the sweeter. Wine *was* sweet, wasn't it?

If Johnny were here he'd be chiding her, "You think too much."

Then they would kiss more. . . .

"Miss Grace was up the other day, asking about you," Mama said.

"Was she?" Willa squirmed a little, realizing how much she'd ignored her friend. Just a few weeks ago she couldn't have imagined being away from the Mission more than a few days at a time, but now that she was making her own stories with Johnny, it was hard to find the time for everything. "It's just that I've been busy."

"I told her how hard you was working." Mama picked up the sewing for real now; Willa watched lazily as the needle flashed through Seraphina's red dress. The too-long hem was tattered and Mama was taking it up a few inches.

Willa wondered if Johnny would like her in a red dress. . . .

A few yards away, someone hollered. Although Willa couldn't make out the words over the driving rain, Mama had heard something, for she'd thrown the clothing into a pile and stood at the edge of the porch, her face drawn and pale in the yellow-gray light.

The men were nearly home before Willa saw them. But she too rose in time to see Ves practically pulling Daddy up the muddy path for the Lowells'; she watched as her father stumbled up the steps and stood there before his wife.

"I've come home to you, Esther," he gasped out, his voice that of an old man. Then he pitched forward, felled like a great tree, collapsing into Mama's waiting arms.

If Willa had lived the last few weeks as if in a dream, she certainly was wide awake now, every day a nightmare. She couldn't close her eyes without hearing Daddy in the other room—coughing, coughing, coughing. Through the thin walls, she could hear him retching into what had once been one of the water pails. Willa once made the mistake of glancing in it as Mama hauled it out to the outhouse, and seeing the swill had nearly made her lose her own stomach. No one in the Lowell family would ever use the bucket for water again, Willa knew, but she scraped it with a nail, carving out a rusting *X*, needing to see the warning.

The house stank with a foul odor.

Every shirt that Daddy wore, every sheet upon his bed, every stringy handkerchief, all were spotted with his blood.

There was still the harvest work. Willa moved from task to task like a sleepwalker, her eyelids fluttering, her fingers thick. Ves joined them in the fields, and Willa was not altogether unhappy he was there. How could she explain to Johnny all that was going on at home? But now was the time she longed for his kisses most; she wished she could throw her arms around him, hiding her face in his shoulder where his very being would block out the sun. The late August heat scorched the earth, the dust rising in clouds about them. Sometimes feeling as though she was choking to death, Willa would clutch at her throat, guessing that this is what her father felt as he fought to draw each wheezing breath.

Granny Maylie came to the cabin again, wandering silently from room to room. "I can give him something to soothe," she told Mama. "But he's beyond my caring."

"We're much obliged," Mama whispered, her own face so white the shadows beneath her eyes shimmered shiny and deep. Once she went over to the crock and handed

Granny a dollar bill. Willa felt a flash of dismay—a whole dollar! And she'd admitted that she couldn't cure him! But of course it was necessary if it would make Daddy more comfortable.

Miss Grace visited—Willa found her standing alone by the stove, her elegant hands clasped before her, praying words so low and quickly that Willa couldn't make them out. When Miss Grace heard her footfall at the door she looked up and smiled, and Willa knew that no matter how standoffish she had been, nothing had really changed between them. "Your hair is growing back," was the first thing Miss Grace said.

Willa put her hand to her head. The hair fell along her neck now, the skin beneath tanned the same brown color. There wasn't any way to call it curly, but it wasn't quite as stick straight as it had once been. Willa tried to be strong but her chin wobbled like a baby's head. "This once seemed so important," she said. When Miss Grace came over and hugged her, Willa leaned into her, breathing in her clean starchy scent, resting more in that moment than she had in a week.

One afternoon Willa came home to find a strange man standing on the porch—a great round giant so pink and wide with health that even his shadow seemed tinted red. He nodded as he passed. "Who is he?" Willa asked Mama when she went inside.

"A doctor, from over Blacksville," Mama told her. "Miss Grace arranged for him to come."

"What did he say?"

"That we have to wait and see."

So they waited. The doctor came every few days, and more than once Willa saw Mama lift the crock to take out a few of the precious bills. Slowly, especially after the nights began to cool, her daddy coughed less and less. He never lost the cough altogether, and in all his life he never would, but the infection passed, leaving him as weak as Rusty. The two would often play together, Rusty handing his father pieces of colored string taken from an old round tin that Mama had once used to keep her quilt pieces in, back when there was fabric enough to piece. Willa watched the dangling threads waver in her father's long thin hands.

By early September there were only the apples left to pick, and Willa was home more and more. She and Seraphina finished the canning. Late one evening Willa chopped the last of the tiny green tomatoes into chunks for relish and tried to tell herself how delicious this last bit of summer would taste during winter's chill. She should take pride in her work—and she did, counting the shiny glass jars and noting the food within each one—but there was no hiding from the stark truth. Even with Ves helping near the end there was not as much this year, and the family had one more mouth to feed. Too many jars would never be filled.

But at least there was the money. They would go into winter with all that Mama had saved, plus whatever Daddy and Ves had earned and never had time to send in the mail. Not as much as there might have been—Willa recalled the doctor's visits—but there would be something.

Glancing at the closed door where her mother was napping with Daddy, Willa tiptoed over to the stove and reached up to the shelf where the crock was kept. Slowly, trying to make no noise, she lifted it down and removed the lid, her eyes widening at what she saw.

Empty.

Ves found her up on the mountain; he'd been coming in just as she dropped the crock. It rolled across the floor with a sound as hollow as Willa felt. Willa didn't bother to pick it up; if she didn't start running she might start screaming and she wasn't sure she would be able to stop. No, she knew she wouldn't. So she ran.

She was sitting on the slab of limestone, her legs tucked up against her body, rocking herself like a cradle. Her head rested on her knees and her eyes were tightly closed. When someone touched her shoulder, she almost said, "Johnny!" before she saw that it was only Ves.

"I figured I might find you here," he said, sitting down beside her. He gazed out over the valley turned gold and green in the setting sun. "Most beautiful sight I've ever seen." He rubbed his eyes as though he couldn't quite believe it. "Down in Hawk's Nest, I used to wonder if I would ever sit here again with you. It was so bad, Willa. I never knew anything in my life like it. Men going into the tunnel knowing they may never come out again. Each morning the guards came through and gathered up the bodies of men who died in their beds, their mouths bloody where the dust had eaten through their lungs and drowned them."

Willa kept rocking. She wanted to tell Ves to stop, to be quiet, but she couldn't find the strength to speak and rock too.

"It was colored men, mostly, up from the south. The bosses were more respectful of Daddy, on account that he was white." He gave a low, ugly laugh. "But the rest of us, we young ones and colored workers, there were hundreds more where we came from. I watched men dump bodies over the side of the mountain—once the dumping was my chore for the day. I . . . I ran off, Willa. That's the only reason you don't hear me in there with him, coughing the innards out of my head."

Willa went still.

"You remember that night last fall, when we sat here talking about Mama? You seemed to grow up that night— all my life I'd thought of you as this kid, and that night you changed. I used to take comfort that you was back here, doing your part. And you did, didn't you? Bet you never once let Mama down."

Willa turned her head to look at him. There were tears running down his cheeks.

"I'll never forgive myself," he told her. "I never will."

"You left Daddy." It was not a question, and Ves didn't bother to answer, not even to nod his head.

"Come on, Willa," he said, his voice pleading. "Don't look at me like that. You can't possibly know. . . ."

"You just told me," she pointed out.

"But even so . . ." Ves dropped his eyes, wiping them with the back of his hand. "It was more awful than I can ever say." Willa couldn't take her eyes off of him. "But listen," he said, his voice eager to make amends. "While I was gone, I went to some of the coal camps down on the Kanawha. I was talking to some union organizers and they say Mr. Roosevelt . . ."

Willa jumped to her feet. "Don't you speak about your Mr. Roosevelt to me," she shouted at him. "Don't you even say his name." All of the anger she had held back—waiting for the time when the mines would open, when Mama would be well, when Mr. Roosevelt would be elected, when Daddy would be home—all this time she had waited for a future to come to pass, only it never did; there was only *now*, and in this *now* there was nothing left.

Ves stared up at her, his mouth open.

"All last year you babbled on . . . Mr. Roosevelt this, Mr. Roosevelt that." She made her voice high and squeaky, not at all like her brother's, but he still winced at her mocking tone. "Look at us, Ves." Willa grabbed his shoulders in her hands and turned him around with such strength that he actually tumbled about before steadying himself. "Look at *this* side of the mountain." From here the ruins of Riley Mines had left the hillside bare. "Your precious Mr. Roosevelt doesn't even know that we're alive!"

From the edge of the tree line came a snap. Both Willa and Ves froze, and watched the silhouette of a man take shape from the shadows.

Ves recognized him first. "Hey, Johnny," he said. There was no mistaking the relief in his voice.

"Hello," Johnny answered, his eyes going back and forth from brother to sister. "I heard someone yelling."

Willa swallowed hard. "It was just me," she told him. "But it weren't anything." You liar, she thought to herself, her hands clenched.

He nodded. "You all right?"

Willa couldn't—wouldn't—lie a second time. She said nothing.

Ves walked over to where Johnny was, and tapped him on the shoulder. "She's had a rough day," he said, looking over his shoulder at her. "She's entitled to some peace and quiet." He headed down toward town, but Johnny didn't join him.

"You coming?" Ves called back.

"Actually," Johnny said, "I came up here to see Willa."

For one heartbeat of a moment, the whole world went still. Ves was now the one looking from one to the other.

"We've sort of been getting to know each other, while you was gone," Johnny said. He walked over and put his arm around Willa.

"I see," Ves said. He kept staring at them as if they were strangers. Despite her anger, Willa felt a wave of pity for her brother who stood there all alone. "I'll be going then," he said, the words sounding as though they were being pulled out one at a time. Then, with a jerk, he crashed through the underbrush for the path that led to town. He did not look back.

As soon as he was gone, Willa turned to Johnny and burst into tears. He took her into his arms, murmuring soothing sounds in her ears, kissing the top of her head. All the fears Willa had kept inside of her since Daddy and Ves had come home came pouring out, not in words, but in great sobs that seemed to turn her inside out, leaving her raw and exposed in the evening air.

Johnny put his hand on her head, pressing her wet face against his damp shirt. "I love you, Willa Lowell," he said. "You know that, don't you?"

Willa nodded, quieter now. The crying had been like a storm blowing through her. But something, perhaps the way that Johnny spoke, told her that more changes were brewing in the air. She could feel the hairs on her arms rise, as if lightning was on its way.

"I've been thinking. I got a brother up in Pittsburgh—he's working on the barges. It's not steady work, but it pays well when they get it. If we was to get married, I could take you away from all this. We could make a fresh start."

Marriage. Willa should have been surprised, but she wasn't. Somewhere in the back of her mind she'd known this was coming. She was nearly seventeen, after all, and Johnny was two years older. People younger than they married all the time, hightailing it to places like Pittsburgh or Baltimore or Cleveland. There was no denying that the idea filled her with a great wave of relief, as deep and overwhelming as if she'd been standing in a creek during a spring tide. If she let it (so tempting!) this wave would pull her under, take her to a place where she need not think of anyone but herself.

He leaned back and tipped her head to his.

"So what do you think, my lady?"

Willa softened at the pet name—he'd taken it from Tennyson's "The Lady of Shalott." She was about to say yes—yes! When inside her head (she was thinking too much again—the curse upon her?) came a voice so clear she could hardly bear to listen:

"You left Daddy."

How could she leave him—leave them all—just yet? Would that be any less a betrayal than what Ves had done?

But I don't want to stay; at first she thought she'd cried this out, but she knew she'd said nothing when Johnny nervously began to tease. "Don't tell me I've gone and said the one thing that makes you speechless."

"Would you do something for me?" she asked him.

"Of course," he said, worried now; this was no answer.

She took his hand and led him inside the stones of the cabin. "Would you stay with me—here? Tonight?" Willa knelt down, feeling the long grass bend beneath them, smooth and soft as any bed she'd ever known. "It will be like all of those afternoons we played you were the pioneer and I was your wife. Only this time will be better because it won't be just pretend. You just have to promise that you'll hold me all night; that you won't let me go."

"You sure?" he asked. He stretched out on the ground.

"Yes," Willa answered. "But only if you promise."

"I promise," he told her, opening his arms. Willa went to him and lay down, listening to the beat of his heart and the shrill cry of the katydids calling from tree to tree.

Chapter Fourteen

After Johnny's proposal, Willa found herself shy and nervous around him. Not that she cared about him any less—indeed, she found herself thinking about him and their lives together all the more. Many mornings she woke up convinced that she would tell him yes, they would get married, and they would leave for Pittsburgh that very day. She wasn't used to city life, but that was part of what made it all the more exciting. Willa knew she was strong—she'd proven this to herself and to Johnny over and over this summer. If there was work to do, she could find a way to do it.

If there was work; it was the "if" that mattered so much.

She was relieved when the coal operators came in late September and opened up the mines for a few weeks, not only because it meant work for the men but also because it kept Johnny too busy to push. He and Ves and Daddy worked every hour that they could, and talk around Riley took on the familiar language of the mines that Willa had grown up speaking: "buying short" and "selling long"—the weight of each man's tonnage depended upon the company's scale which might be rigged one way or the other, but never to the benefit of those who went deep underground. Before each workday, teams of men walked through the "rooms" of the mines in their heads, noting every pillar of coal, every seam where it snaked through the tunnels like a shiny underground stream. Forgetting a forest of blackened ancient trees when dynamiting might mean a cave-in, a broken leg, or a crushed back. There was concern about "pulling pillars," which meant taking out the very foundations of the mine itself, but it was cheaper than blasting through the mountain. With the chance to work, the men were familiar again in their dusty skins, but their womenfolk went from worrying about the lack of money to the anxiety of sending their men down into the earth, always listening with one ear for the whistle that might mean the worst possible news.

Even with the mines open, there was no gaiety about it as there had been last year with the election coming on. Everyone knew the busy time would be short and sweet— just enough to sink your teeth into before winter came and the companies pulled out again. Watching Daddy step into his boots every morning and pull on his work clothes always sent a chill down Willa's spine. He was better now than he had been, but he tired too quickly; he coughed too much.

"You got no business going down in," Ves insisted. "You'll come out with black lung if you ain't careful."

Willa dreaded black lung—the coal dust settled into the miner's lung until you could hear every death-rattle breath. After what Daddy had been through this summer, they all knew the risk was greater.

"This is still my family," Daddy told Ves. "It's my job to take care of you." He picked up a biscuit and dipped it into an egg Mama had fried. Willa wasn't sure if Mama was buying the eggs on credit, knowing there would be scrip coming to use in the company store, but she was glad to get them. With just a little salt, the eggs tasted delicious, and no one in the Lowell family left a drop of yolk lingering on the plate.

"You go and catch pneumonia—"

"That's enough, Ves," Mama interrupted, patting him on the shoulder. "Eat your breakfast and leave your father be." But her own hands weren't so steady as she poured Daddy another cup of coffee.

"Yes'm," Ves muttered. Willa sympathized with her brother's feelings, but she knew that if she were in

Daddy's place she would go too. As would Ves.

With Johnny working late and her own mood swinging back and forth, Willa was glad to spend her evenings in the Mission. When she sat in the comfy chairs reading poetry, Willa could pretend it was springtime, when anything might be possible, and not the edges of another winter with its cold and pinching hunger.

Roselia often joined her. As close as the two girls were, they enjoyed reading different things. "Listen to this, Willa," Roselia would say, and then read something like Lewis Carroll's "Jabberwocky." Roselia delighted in the nonsense of words, the very silliness of language to mean everything and nothing. Of course, with their parents, Roselia and Theresa spoke in a mixture of Italian and English, the foreign words sounding no less strange than the "brillig and slithy toves" to Willa's untrained ear.

Willa found herself turning to poems for strength, for a way of helping her sort out her whirling feelings:

> *If you can dream—and not make*
> *dreams your master;*
> *If you can think—and not make*
> *thoughts your aim;*
> *If you can meet with Triumph and*
> *Disaster*

And treat these two imposters as the
same. . . .

Surely, Willa told herself, if I could just memorize enough words, if I could put them in the right order, I would figure out just what I'm supposed to do.

But there was the word "if" again, down to the name of the poem itself.

One night Willa lingered at the Mission, waiting for even Roselia to go home so she could talk privately with Miss Grace. When Ves came down and offered to walk her home, Willa told him she wasn't ready yet. "But you might take Roselia," she said, remembering how, back in Fairmont, Roselia had called Ves handsome.

"Okay. Sure." He didn't sound very excited about it.

"Unless it's too much trouble," Roselia said. Willa had to keep from rolling her eyes—Roselia lived in the first row of cabins and Ves would walk right by them. How much trouble could it be?

"It's no trouble," he said, smiling at Roselia, who turned pink and pretty. "I suppose Johnny's coming for you or something." He tried to make his voice teasing, but Willa knew he wasn't yet comfortable knowing that his best friend was courting his sister.

"Or something," Willa replied vaguely, watching them go. Roselia bent her head and laughed at whatever Ves was saying. Since he'd come back from Hawk's Nest, Ves had been edgy and skittish, ready to jump out of his own skin. Maybe a girl like Roselia could help settle him down.

"Something on your mind?" Miss Grace asked. She locked the door and pulled the curtain over the picture window.

"Do you ever think about getting married?"

Miss Grace didn't even blink at the sudden question. "I've had two proposals," she said, her voice even.

"But you aren't married," Willa pointed out.

"So my mother keeps reminding me," Miss Grace said with a laugh.

"Johnny asked me to marry him."

"I see."

When Miss Grace said nothing more, Willa wished she'd never brought it up at all. She squirmed in her chair which suddenly seemed to have grown lumps and bumps that pressed uncomfortably into her skin.

"I don't know what to tell him. There's a part of me that wants to go—I like being with Johnny. But there's a part of me that feels like I'm not ready yet, at least not ready for marriage and maybe babies and all the things that go into it. Either way, I feel like I'll look back someday and wonder if I made the right choice."

"'Of all the words of tongue and pen, the saddest are what might have been,'" Miss Grace quoted.

"Is that from a poem?" Willa asked.

Miss Grace shook her head. "It's just a saying, I'm afraid."

"Oh. Sort of like 'married in black, you'll wish yourself back'?" Willa grinned. "And here's me with a gray dress; maybe that means even my dress can't make up its mind!"

Miss Grace refused to be distracted. "I don't think there is any way we can not look back and question whether we did the right thing. The only thing I know to do is to make sure that no matter what choices I make, I chose to do something worth doing with my life."

Willa gestured to the book she'd been reading. "I know. 'If you can fill each unforgiving moment with sixty seconds worth of distance run . . .'"

"Then yours is the earth and everything in it," Miss Grace finished for her.

"This leaves me back where I started." The words were as much sighed as spoken.

"I'm afraid so," Miss Grace answered. Then she stood up and walked over to a table and picked up a letter. Willa thought she was going to read it to her—perhaps there was something in it like a poem that would help her make sense of everything. But Miss Grace just put it down without mentioning it.

"Before you decide anything, would you wait a day or

two until you can meet a friend of mine? She's coming to visit and I think you'd like her."

"Is it Miss Ginny?" Willa remembered the woman in Fairmont with the blue eyes.

Miss Grace's eyebrows shot up. "Gin's a dear, but I'd be surprised to see her come all the way out here. No, this guest is someone else altogether. You'll like her."

What on earth could this friend have to do with whether or not she should marry Johnny? But Willa agreed; a few more days wouldn't make any difference.

Almost a week went by before Miss Grace and her guest visited the Lowell cabin. The rooms sparkled with cleanliness; Willa and Mama had scrubbed every morning in case that would be the day. Once, after a few days had passed, Willa had gone down to the Mission only to find it locked up, a sign in the window saying that Miss Grace would return soon.

When the knock finally came, Mama handed Rusty to Willa and went to open the door. "Come in," Mama said. "Come in."

Before Miss Grace could speak, the strange woman with her called out, "Splendid! I've heard so much about your lovely family and I couldn't wait to meet each and every one of you." The woman, so tall she made the cabin seem to shrink all around her, gave Willa a toothy smile.

"This must be Willa, the splendid girl I've been hearing so much about."

Willa tried not to giggle. Miss Grace was right—this woman wasn't at all like Miss Ginny in Fairmont. Her voice was high and birdlike, almost a screeching sound. Still, it was nice to be called splendid, and there was no doubt that the stranger liked what she saw. Willa wished that she could say the same, but as pretty as Miss Ginny had been, this new friend was as homely as could be. Dressed in the same dark blue skirt and white blouse that Miss Grace wore, Willa figured her for a fellow missionary.

"Won't you sit down?" Mama offered the chair, her voice nervous. Willa knew she, too, was wishing there were more than one.

"I'd be delighted to," the woman answered. "But I insist you take the chair. We're the intruders." She held out her arms for Rusty and, to Willa's surprise, the little boy went to her willingly. "Aren't you a darling," she told him, bouncing him on her thin hip. He grabbed for her dark blue hat and pulled it from her head.

"Rusty," Mama scolded.

But the woman only laughed. "Splendid little chap you have here. Makes me think of my own young ones—nearly all grown now."

Now that everything had been deemed splendid,

Mama seemed to come to her senses. "Willa, go and get the Granny quilt for our guests to sit on."

"Don't go to any trouble," the woman started to say, but Mama interrupted.

"You be guests in my home, and I'll offer you what I have."

The tall woman reached out and touched Mama's shoulder. "Bless you, dear."

When Willa came back with the quilt, the woman said, "This is beautiful work. Did you do it, Mrs. Lowell?" She folded her angular body down on the floor. Miss Grace settled in beside her, winking at Willa as though this whole visit was some shared, "splendid" joke between them.

"My mother's," Mama answered. "I never was one for quilting, though with my brood there is plenty of sewing to be done."

"Tell me more about your family. Grace was saying that in addition to our lovely Willa here, you have three boys and another girl?"

The "lovely Willa" worried that the entire camp could hear the woman's voice; they had left the door open for the light and air, and the birdcall surely carried on this quiet afternoon.

"Ves is our oldest," Mama said. "'Course, he's really my husband's boy, but I've raised him as my own. Then Willa, followed by Seraphina and Kyle and the baby, Rusty."

Willa listened to the talk—mostly the woman asking questions and Mama answering them. Johnny's name never came up and although Willa had hoped for an answer, she was also relieved. She hadn't told Mama yet about Johnny proposing; no one knew except Miss Grace.

As the women prepared to leave, the stranger handed Mama back a sleeping Rusty, after placing a kiss on the top of his head. "You have a splendid family, Mrs. Lowell," the woman said.

"Thank you," Mama said. "It was good to meet you, and to see you again, Miss Grace." Willa felt proud that Mama spoke as politely as her guests.

"Do you think we have time to go over to the Hamdens?" Miss Grace asked the woman. Willa pricked up her ears. Why on earth would anyone want to go visiting there? Mrs. Hamden would only sniff; no one was good enough for *her*.

The woman shook her head. "I think we need to go and find out how Bob is doing." Turning back to Mama she said, "A friend of mine joined us, but became ill when we were visiting the Ankers' cabin."

Mama hesitated, and then said, "That's a bad one, all right. But they . . . we . . . we aren't all like that."

Willa watched the woman's eyes go through the cabin one more time. She knew what Mama meant.

When you walked into the Ankers' house, you felt like gagging; bugs crawled on the floor, over the beds, about the stove. Willa would rather Mama clean too much than too little.

"I can see that you aren't," the woman said. She smiled at everyone one last time and gave Willa's shoulder a squeeze. "You keep on being such a splendid girl," she said. She bent down to Willa's ear. "And believe in your dreams, child. Believe."

"I'll try," Willa whispered back, wondering if this was supposed to mean something—and if so, what? (There was that word "if" again!) She stood beside Mama and watched the women walk down the hill to the village. Though plain, their bright blue skirts made a brilliant splash against the grays and browns of the company town. The new missionary chattered on, her arms waving like a pinwheel.

Ves was coming up as they were going down. Willa saw him stop and stare, until the women had passed from sight. Then he turned and ran up the hillside as fast as he could.

"Who was that?" he asked, so out of breath he panted.

"Shhh! Don't you go and wake up Rusty," Mama said. "I'll never get supper started if he wakes up yelling."

"But who was that?" Ves had lowered his voice but Willa could hear the excitement in it.

"A friend of Miss Grace's," Willa said. She realized that they didn't know the woman's name. "Probably someone from Fairmont."

"That woman isn't from Fairmont," Ves said.

"How would you know?"

Ves looked first at her, then at Mama. "'Cause unless I miss my guess, that woman is Mrs. Roosevelt." Willa stared at him. Mama stared at him. "Eleanor Roosevelt—the president's wife."

Willa started to laugh, but stopped. The idea was ridiculous, of course—even for one so taken with the Roosevelts as Ves was. No president's wife was ever going to come to Riley Mines.

But there had been something about the strange woman that Willa couldn't quite put her finger on.

Mama smoothed her hair. In the early autumn light it shone silvery again, after seeming gray almost a whole year. "Good gracious me" was all that Mama said.

"Who?" Daddy asked that night when he came home.

"Mrs. Roosevelt," Willa answered. She had answered this question three times now and knew that Daddy still didn't believe her.

"Did she say she was Mrs. Roosevelt?" Freshly scrubbed from the mines, his skin was pale and bare looking.

"Well, no," Willa admitted. "But Ves said she was."

"Well," Daddy said. "If Ves said she was, then that explains it." He grinned at Mama.

"Really, Waitman," Mama said. She placed a plate of buckwheat cakes down in front of him. Willa could smell the tangy sourness of the batter as Mama cooked up another batch. Although Willa had eaten her share of the hot cakes at dinner, her stomach grumbled. Daddy poured molasses over them and rolled them up.

"Ves is always getting ahead of himself," Daddy said, eating the cakes as fast as Mama could flip them on his plate.

"I think he's on to something," Mama said. "He seemed so sure, for one thing."

Daddy snorted. "Leave it to you womenfolk to get all worked up about a man being sure."

"Happens so rarely," Mama teased.

He laughed. "Now let's get down to the facts of the matter. First, does anyone here know what Mrs. Roosevelt looks like?"

"You know we don't," Mama protested. "Only newspapers around here are too old to be of much account."

"I've heard she's awful homely," Willa added. "And if you had seen the woman, you would have to call her homely." She paused. "But she had the kindest eyes, Daddy. You just felt better when she was there, homely or not."

"Doesn't sound like a president's wife to me," Daddy said. "And where did you hear that she was homely? You reading the city papers?"

"No," she answered.

"So where'd you hear it?" Daddy asked again.

Willa didn't want to answer. She looked over at Mama, whose mouth twitched. "Ves told me," Willa said after a minute.

Daddy roared.

Mama joined in until Daddy started coughing so bad that his eyes ran and he had to blow his nose. Willa saw small spots of red blood when he took the handkerchief away from his mouth.

"Best be lying down," he murmured. He stood up and headed for the bed, his tall, lean body tumbling into it. The crash woke Rusty in the other room.

Mama knelt by Daddy. "Go check the baby for me," she told Willa.

"Yes, Mama." Willa was glad enough to have an excuse to go. The echo of Daddy's cough followed her.

Chapter Fifteen

Willa jumped when, a few days later, there was another knock at their door. "Good heavens," Mama fussed, after a glance out the window. "It's your Miss Grace again." She tried to straighten up the room; not that it was messy, but unless Mama had been cleaning all day, the cabin would never be good enough for company. When Willa answered, she saw her friend was not alone. Two men stood with her, dressed in dark suits like company men. What was Miss Grace doing with company men? Willa felt her stomach clench. There was only one answer: something had happened to Daddy or Ves.

Mama obviously feared the same thing. "What's going on?" she asked, moving Willa out of the way and standing before the door as though guarding it.

"Can we come in?" Miss Grace asked. She must have seen the look on Mama's face because she smiled and held up her hands. "It's nothing to worry you, Mrs. Lowell. We'd just like to ask a few questions."

What questions? Willa felt panicky. Company men meant only bad news. Perhaps they had decided that Daddy wasn't strong enough; miners were often evicted when they could no longer work.

"Willa," Mama called back to her. "I want you to take your brothers and head down to the Olivettis'. Heaven knows where Seraphina's off to, but if you find her, you keep her with you. Don't you come until I fetch you."

"It's not what you think . . . ," Miss Grace started to say.

"But Mama . . . ," Willa said at the same time.

Mama shook her head. "No matter why you're here, I can't change it. But I ask you to let Willa go." She looked down at her daughter. "You do as I say."

"Of course," Miss Grace said. "But I promise that this is only about happy news. . . ."

"And I'll be glad to listen to you and answer your questions just as soon as my Willa and the boys leave."

Willa knew that voice; her mother would accept no argument. She looked up at Miss Grace and hoped that her eyes would let her friend know that she trusted her. Then she gathered up Rusty and headed down the mountain, Kyle almost dragging behind her.

* * *

"There was an old man in the North Country, bow down. . . ."

Willa could hear Mama singing long before she reached the Lowell house. The music seemed to float down the mountainside, filling the spaces between the dingy company homes and spreading into the valley below.

"I thought you said the men were there," Ves said. He too had stopped climbing the path and stood and listened.

"They were." Scared as she was, Willa liked hearing the music. Mama hadn't sung for so long she'd almost forgotten the sound of it.

"He gave to his love a golden ring, bow down. . . ."

"You think she's gone stark out of her mind?" Ves asked.

Willa glared at Ves. "Mama isn't in the habit of going crazy."

"She ain't in the habit of talking to company men, neither," Ves shot back. "They come and tell her that something happened to Daddy, well, anything could happen."

Ves was right—how did she know that Mama hadn't heard something awful about Daddy? Men died in the mines all of the time. Just because she hadn't heard an explosion or seen the women running for the mouth of the mine didn't mean that the worst hadn't happened, no matter what Miss Grace had said.

"I will be true, true to my love, love if my love will be true to me. . . ."

"I won't believe that until I talk to Mama," Willa said. "You know that's the 'Twa Sisters,' and Mama only sings that when she's happy."

"Either way, best get it over with," Ves said and climbed the steps two at a time.

When she saw Mama sitting in the chair with her hands folded on her lap, Willa almost lost it; Mama never sat with her hands folded. But the expression on her face matched the joyous singing, not the stillness. "You won't believe what Miss Grace said," she told them, practically hugging herself.

"What about the men in suits?" Ves interrupted. "What did they want with us?"

"You won't believe it," Mama repeated almost dreamily. Then she seemed to catch herself. "What time is your Daddy done with his shift today?" she asked Ves.

"About eight," Ves said.

Willa couldn't wait anymore. "I'm heading down to Miss Grace's," she said. If Mama wouldn't talk, surely her friend would.

"The only place you're going, young lady, is to the Olivettis', to pick up your brothers. I believe I told you that you were to stay until I came for you?" Mama's voice wasn't angry, just firm.

Willa felt her face get warm. "I didn't mean to disobey," she said. "And I did find Seraphina." There was no need to tell Mama that Sera had been playing in the creek again; given how much time she spent there, Willa couldn't help but wonder if her sister wasn't part fish.

"You needn't have run off to fetch Ves," Mama said. "Now, if you both hurry, you can be back before your daddy gets home."

She started humming again.

Even when the whole family was together, Mama pretended nothing had happened. Finally Daddy couldn't take it. "Out with it, Esther," he said. "These kids are gonna be the death of me, they're squirming so."

Mama laughed. "They've been nervous nellies since the men were here today."

Daddy sat straight up. "What men?"

"The government men," Mama answered, her eyes wide, her voice innocent.

"Government men?" Ves said in surprise. He turned to Willa. "You said they were company men."

"They were wearing suits," Willa told him. "And if men in suits show up at the door . . ."

"Willa's right," Mama interrupted. "I took them for company men at first, too. That's why I sent her down to the Olivettis'." Willa was glad that Mama hadn't mentioned that she had not obeyed that afternoon; Daddy would not be happy to hear that, no matter what the news from the government men.

"So, Esther," Daddy said, "are you going to tell us about these government men or just leave us in suspense?"

Mama sat back on the bedding, rocking Rusty back and forth. Kyle climbed into Daddy's lap. "The men were from the Roosevelt administration—friends of the first lady. And that was Mrs. Roosevelt who visited here." She looked directly at Daddy, whose mouth dropped open. "Seems the president has set up a new town for people like us—people who can't make enough in the mines to get out of these coal camps. When Mrs. Roosevelt was here, she was looking for families that might want to go settle in these new towns, away from the mines."

"Away from the mines?" Ves asked. "Why would we want to do that?"

"Can't pay our bills without the mines," Daddy agreed. "Even a little work is better than charity."

"It's not charity," Mama insisted. "We'd work just the same as we do here but for a lot more. The government leases us a house and some land—enough to plant a garden and maybe even have a cow and chickens. It would be like being back at the homeplace." Mama's eyes grew soft; she kissed Rusty's red hair. "The children could go to school."

Willa held her breath; did "children" mean just the little ones?

"So how would we pay for this bounty given to us by Mr. Roosevelt?" Daddy asked. Willa could tell he didn't believe Mama. She wasn't sure that she did either.

Mama placed Rusty's cheek against her own. "That's the best part, Wait. They're gonna start a factory there. Maybe even a wood shop. I told Mrs. Roosevelt that you were good with your hands—that you'd made the chair you're sitting in now."

"A wood shop," Daddy echoed. He looked down at his hands. In the faint light of the lamp, Willa could make out the half-moons of coal dust that never left the ridges in Daddy's fingernails.

"Seems Mrs. Roosevelt has a liking for chairs—some Quakers came in a coal camp and taught the men how to make these special chairs. Mrs. Roosevelt bought one and got interested when she heard it was unemployed miners making them. Miss Grace said that people like the Roosevelts had been hearing from coal operators for years about how shiftless and stupid people were in the mines, but when Mrs. Roosevelt saw this chair, she knew that no lazy man had ever made something so beautiful."

"She knew all that from a chair?" Daddy asked. He was still skeptical, but Willa could tell that he wanted to be convinced.

"You'd have to meet her to understand," Mama said. This time she turned to Willa. "Mrs. Roosevelt is a most uncommon woman."

"She's right, Daddy," Willa chimed in. "No matter how bad you know everything is, when she's talking to you, you start to think that maybe it ain't so bad after all."

"A wood shop," Daddy said again.

"And a house, with a garden and chickens and maybe even a cow." Mama jumped up, making Rusty bolt awake. "Think of it, Wait. We could start fresh without taking on debt at the company store or struggling in this old shack."

Daddy stood, Kyle almost asleep in his arms. "I can't think of it all," he said. "Maybe tomorrow, after I've taken it all in. Right now it's just too much for this old man." He headed to put his son to bed.

Willa looked over at Ves. "What do you think?" she whispered.

"I like the cow," Sera piped up.

"Don't know," he muttered. "Never dreamed we'd be leaving the mines."

"You're the one said things would get better when Roosevelt was elected," Willa reminded him.

Mama interrupted. "Off to bed, you three. Those men are coming here tomorrow afternoon to talk to all of us, so there will be plenty to do."

"Did you hear the part about a cow?" Seraphina asked

as they lay down, the straw crunching beneath them. Willa listened to Sera rattle off every kind of barnyard animal. The prattle was soothing; Willa was just about to fall asleep when she woke up long enough to remember that she hadn't thought about Johnny or Pittsburgh the whole day.

Willa woke before dawn. She knew that there would be buckets and buckets of water to be brought to the house. "Wake up." Willa shook Seraphina's arm.

"Go away," Sera muttered and rolled over. She wrapped the blanket around her shoulders. Willa shivered in the cold autumn air and hurried to dress, wishing her stockings weren't quite so full of holes. No one's going to be looking at your legs, she reminded herself, but the gaps nagged at her. Maybe if she hurried this morning, there would be a chance to put a few darns in.

Only Mama was up; she stood on the porch watching the sunrise over the eastern ridge. "You're up early," Willa said, breaking the quiet.

"I just came out to make sure we were going to have a nice day," Mama said. She put her hands on her arms and rubbed them.

"You were praying, weren't you?" Willa asked. She stared up at the sky. In the early light, the valley looked dirty and gray, but above the mountain was a streak of pale blue.

"I might have been," Mama answered. "Though I didn't know I was until you mentioned it."

"Do you think it's real?" Willa asked. Everything was happening so fast. She could hardly believe that this time yesterday she hadn't even known the government men existed.

Mama kept watching the sunrise. The light grew stronger; the sky turned deep blue. "It has to be, Willa. It just has to."

By noon, Willa had scrubbed the walls and floor until no trace of coal dust could be seen. Over and over she emptied the bucket of its oily black water and trudged down the hill to the spigot. After a brief dinner of biscuits spread with bacon fat, Willa gave Rusty, then Kyle, and finally herself as much of a bath as she could manage. She built a roaring fire in the stove to keep the place warm. Then she went down the mountain once more for fresh water. Her back ached and the muscles in her legs cramped, but Willa was surprised to note that she wasn't tired; those weeks of work on the farm had toughened her as housework never had.

Miss Grace arrived at three. She said the government man, named Mr. Frey, was right behind her. "He'll be asking you questions," she told them. "Questions about your family, and what you know about farming and such."

"Esther told me it was to be a factory," Daddy said anxiously. He wore his dark work pants and the sweater Willa had brought him from Fairmont. His thin hair was damp around his ears. "I don't know much about farming."

"There is a factory, and no doubt Mr. Frey will want to ask you about that too," Miss Grace assured him.

"I grew up on a farm," Mama said. "And Ves and Willa here have worked on one, as has Wait. Surely that will qualify us." Her eyes roamed around the cabin looking for something to do; she kept folding and unfolding the Granny quilt, her hands unable to keep still.

"You're all going to do fine," Miss Grace told them.

Footsteps thundered on the porch; the Lowells glanced at each other. Willa felt a lump in her stomach, but then a chill went through her, blowing the fogginess from her mind until she felt as clear and sharp as a cold winter's night. This keen awareness was almost painful, as the questions dragged on and on. Willa sat by the stove next to Kyle, watching the man scribble little marks with a pencil on a sheet of paper. Every time he reached the bottom of the page, Willa was sure that this would be the end, but he kept turning the pages over and asking more questions. Some seemed rather stupid.

"Can you tell a rooster from a hen?" he asked Daddy.

"Yes, sir."

"Can you describe the difference?" The man did not look up.

"Well," Daddy said, "a hen is a girl chicken. It lays eggs." Frantic, he looked over at Mama, who nodded encouragingly. "A rooster is a male chicken and has a comb and a fluffy tail. . . ." His voice trailed off. Willa decided the answer wasn't as easy as she'd thought; everyone knew the difference between a hen and a rooster, but putting that difference into words was difficult. "Hen lays eggs," Daddy added, "and a rooster don't."

"Quite so," the man said. He made more notes with his pencil.

"Now, Mrs. Lowell. Are you familiar with canning and other food storage procedures?"

"Yes, sir," Mama answered. Willa had to strain to hear Mama's voice, but the words came easily enough. Mama talked knowledgeably about not only canning but also smoking meat and curing hams.

"Very good, Mrs. Lowell." The man made more notes and turned the page over. "Now, the next questions are somewhat more difficult, and sometimes a little personal. Try and be as honest as you can."

"I will, sir." The dignity in Daddy's voice caught the man's attention at last. Willa felt very proud that this man did not cow her father.

"I see that," the government man said with a small

smile. Then he looked back at the paper. "You were both native born?"

Daddy nodded but Mama looked startled. "Wait here was born in Monongalia County," she said, "as were all the children. I was born over in Farmington—that would be Marion County." Her words were careful and precise.

"That's fine," the man said. Still writing, he asked, "Can you verify your marriage information?"

Mama and Daddy looked at each other. "Just what do you be implying?" Daddy asked. He took Mama's hand; for the first time, Mama looked scared.

Miss Grace touched Mama's shoulder. "He just needs to know that you are legally wed—by a minister, or a justice of the peace."

"Oh," Mama said, her body going limp with relief. "I have the license from the courthouse." She stood up and pulled out a piece of paper from a tin.

The man glanced at it and made more notes. "Waitman Lowell and Esther Kerns . . . ," he muttered. "And these are all your children? Let me see, Sylvester, Willa, Seraphina, Kyle, and Russell?" He barely glanced at them.

"Yes, sir," Daddy answered. "Now, Ves here is my first wife's boy, but Esther has raised him as her own and he regards her as his mama, don't you, boy?" he said.

"Yes, Daddy," Ves said. Willa could see the circles of

red form on Ves's cheeks. He sounded so stilted and false, when Willa knew just how true it was.

The strange man didn't seem to notice. "Do you drink, Mr. Lowell?" he asked.

"No, sir," Daddy said. "My pap was a preacherman."

The man eyed him over his glasses, his pencil poised over the form. "Those are often the worst ones," he said wryly.

Daddy nodded. "And I'm not claiming that I'm a saint, and I've had a drop or two in my time, but I can say to you that I'm not a drinker. If you like, I can take the temperance pledge right now."

The man waved this away. "No need, no need." He made a few more scribbles and then finally flipped the pages closed. "Normally we get a reference from someone at this time—often a minister, or a family member in good standing in the community." Willa could see the shiny patches on his suit where his elbows jutted, round as doorknobs. When she looked closely, she could just make out the dark patch along his cuff. This man isn't rich at all, Willa realized, and from that moment on, she was less afraid.

"You folks have had the good fortune of a reference from Mrs. Roosevelt herself, not to mention Miss McCartney here." He held out his hand to Daddy. "You are to be congratulated."

Daddy took the hand, but looked puzzled. "Does that mean we can go?" he asked.

The man pumped Daddy's hand and smiled. Willa decided he was rather nice looking; his smile made him look very young. "That's right," he said.

Mama made a small sound in the back of her throat. Daddy's face creased into a grin so broad his eyes buttoned up and nearly disappeared. "You hear that, Esther?" Tears ran down Mama's cheeks; she picked up Rusty and gathered him to her, hiding her tears in his little body.

Miss Grace came over and hugged Willa. "I'm so happy about this," she told her. Willa looked over at Ves, who was more shell-shocked than anything else. Seraphina was jumping up and down. "Where are we going, again?" she demanded.

"It's called Arthurdale," Miss Grace told her. "It's a lovely place—you will have a house to live in and a big yard with a garden. You can go to school and your daddy can work in the factory there."

"When are we going?" she asked.

"As soon as you can."

Chapter Sixteen

On a cold night in late October, Willa waited for Johnny to meet her at the pioneer cabin. More than a month had gone by since they had last been here, when Johnny had asked her to marry him. But as Willa sat on the limestone step and gazed out over the valley, she was struck by just how much this place had come to mean to her; she could hardly believe that barely a year had passed since she'd seen it for the first time.

Then she had come with Ves, on a night very much like this one, with the trees bare of leaves, silhouetted in the moonlight. Rusty had not yet been born and Mama was so ill. Now it was Daddy they fussed over, and Willa was coming to learn that being grown up meant always knowing what could go wrong even when you tried to make it come out right. Still, she wouldn't have traded that moment with Ves for anything; that evening they had grown closer, sharing their fears and desperate hopes.

Willa wouldn't trade the night with Johnny either—
that had been a point in her life when all of the pieces
inside of her had nearly broken apart, like a china cup
dropped upon a hard stone floor. When he had stayed with
her, held her, she had found a way to keep the deepest core
of Willa Lowell from shattering as well. And now, with the
idea of Arthurdale, that despair which had nearly drowned
her was fading as the darkness does with the rising of the
sun.

She heard Johnny before she saw him—he came up the
path from Riley and Willa ran to him. His arms went
around her, and she fell gratefully into the strength of him,
the very warmth of his body which pressed against hers. I'd
never be cold again, if I marry Johnny, Willa thought, lux-
uriating in the familiar way her head snuggled up against his
chin. Maybe it was this shared nearness that kept couples
like Mama and Daddy going, no matter how difficult their
lives became.

It had been so long since they'd last been together that
Willa had expected passionate kisses; she'd thought about
how tightly he would hold her, how he would tell her that
he missed her. Tonight Johnny did none of these things—
he held her, yes, but in a loose, almost casual way that
made her pull back and ask what was wrong.

"When were you going to tell me?" he asked. News

about Arthurdale was all over Riley Mines.

"Tell you what?" He'd been patient, never demanding that she answer his proposal. When she thought about the new settlement town she was glad—not only for her family, but because an immediate answer was no longer so necessary. Now she and Johnny could both go and yet not need to run away; they could be together without leaving everyone else behind.

"I just thought we could wait a bit," she told him. "Maybe save some money—Miss Grace says there will be work for everyone in Arthurdale. That's more sure than even Pittsburgh."

"Yeah, well, you can earn it all yourself, then." Johnny let her go and walked over to the foundation and leaned against it. Willa could hear the stones creaking against his weight.

"What do you mean?" she asked him.

Johnny didn't answer but began throwing rocks down the hillside. At first Willa thought the mortar had worked loose, forming small round pebbles. But when one rock crashed through the underbrush, she realized he was pulling the wall apart.

"Stop!" she called out, rushing over to him. She grabbed his hand, realizing in a new way just how strong he was as he pulled against her. "You'll destroy it."

"What do you care?" he said roughly. "You won't be here to see."

"What's wrong with you? What's the difference between Pittsburgh and Arthurdale so long as there's work and we're together?"

Johnny dropped his arm, the stones falling to the ground. "The difference," he told her, "is that Arthurdale doesn't want me."

"I don't understand," Willa said. "How could a town not want you?"

"When the government men talked to your family about going, what did they ask you? About farming? Did they even bother to ask where you all were born? Or were you friends enough with all the bigwigs like your Miss Grace that they didn't even bother?"

His angry words rained down on Willa, pelting her like the stones he'd thrown away. She'd never seen him so furious, and it scared her a little, though she tried not to let him see. "But you were born here, weren't you? Here in Riley Mines?"

Seeing the anguish on her face made his body relax. "Yeah, but my ma was born in Ireland." He snapped off the word as though it were a curse. "Every one of us was baptized Catholic."

"Oh," Willa said, her body sinking to the earth, down in the gritty dirt which ground into her skin. "But that won't matter. I know it."

Johnny's eyes narrowed. "You know what one of those

government men said while he was getting in the car? They said the Negroes wouldn't make an effort to keep a town nice, and foreigners were even worse."

Willa dropped her head into her hands, wishing the weight of it would push her into the earth itself. She could hear the man in the shiny suit who had sat in the Lowell cabin only a few days ago, asking if everyone in the household was "native born." She hadn't thought about it at the time; she hadn't known how important the question was that he was asking.

"So you can go to your precious Arthurdale and feel better than the likes of us, or you can come to Pittsburgh with me."

If Johnny had been grasping one arm and her family the other, Willa could not have felt more torn in two. "I can't just give up my family like that," she said.

Johnny knelt before her, a hand on either side of her face. "I want to be your family." He leaned forward to kiss her, so eager that his head crashed into her nose.

"Oh, Willa," he cried, when she gasped from the pain. Johnny gently touched her upper lip, his fingers turning black from the blood he found there. "I only meant to kiss you . . . I swear it. You have to know that. I wouldn't hurt you for anything." He sounded horrified.

Willa didn't care about the bleeding. A few drops had fallen on her dress, and she could see the round circles that she knew would be deep red in a clearer light. "I'm going to see Miss Grace," she told him. "She'll fix everything. You wait and see."

The last time Willa had raced up the rickety steps to Miss Grace's rooms above the Mission, a light had been burning. This time, the apartment was dark. But Willa didn't care. She wouldn't have cared if there had been no steps at all; if she'd had to climb the wall with her bare hands, she would have found a way. She banged on her friend's door, calling out, "Miss Grace? It's Willa. I have to talk to you."

When Miss Grace opened the door and saw Willa's bloody face, she became alarmed. "What happened?" she asked, pulling her inside.

Willa wiped the back of her hand over her nose; she didn't care about that. "I have to know something about Arthurdale. When that man came to our cabin and asked us about being native born, did he mean we couldn't go if Mama or Daddy had been born in Ireland, or someplace else like that?" As she spoke, Willa realized that "someplace else" meant Italy too. The Olivettis—Roselia!—would also be left behind.

Miss Grace didn't say anything, only took a washcloth from a box on the floor and wet it with water poured from a white china pitcher. She wrung it out over a bucket and tried to put it against Willa's face, but Willa brushed her aside.

"I need to know," she said, her voice hoarse; the iron taste of blood ran from her nose and down her throat.

"Would you hate me if I told you yes? It's true."

Willa froze. She had never expected this answer from her friend.

"I don't understand," she said. This time, when Miss Grace offered the wet cloth she took it; Willa buried her face in it—pressed it against her burning eyes.

"Do you want to sit down?" Miss Grace went over to the desk and pulled out the straight backed chair. She slipped into her bedroom a moment and came back with another one, equally plain, for herself.

"You know about the Roosevelts?" Miss Grace asked.

Willa sat down. She felt weary and lightheaded, as though she were coming down with the flu. It was hard to focus on what Miss Grace was saying. "I know everyone keeps telling me they want to make the world a better place."

"And they are—Arthurdale is considered Mrs. Roosevelt's pet project in Washington. If we can make it a success, we can build other towns like it that will help thousands of people."

"What about the Settles? And the Olivettis?"

Miss Grace removed her glasses and pinched the bridge of her nose. "The only way Mrs. Roosevelt could get the government to support the Arthurdale project was by agreeing to select only white, native-born settlers. Men and women with families preferably, and Protestant."

"But why?" Willa demanded. "Mr. Roosevelt's the president."

"Believe me, there are plenty in Washington who think that the Roosevelts are doing far more than they should." Miss Grace didn't hide the bitterness she felt. "If it was up to some in Congress, they'd crush every part of the New Deal."

"I still don't understand." Willa wondered how many times she would have to repeat herself.

"Look, Willa, there are people in Congress, people in the state houses, people right here in West Virginia that care about one thing—themselves." Miss Grace leaned in and put her hands on Willa's knees, her grip tightening as she spoke. "And these bigoted, racist, arrogant fools would rather pretend that no one is to blame for the havoc that this Depression has wrought. Ask them if the government couldn't do something, they tell you that it isn't any of the government's business—they'll call you socialist, as if fighting for a decent standard of living for all people isn't part of the equality that the Declaration of Independence was all about."

The last of her words were still ringing in Willa's ears when Miss Grace let go of Willa and sat back, a faint smile on her lips. "I can get carried away on this subject," she muttered.

"I always thought you'd make a great preacher," Willa said.

Miss Grace put her hands to her face, which had gone beet red. "I'm sorry," she started to say, but Willa cut her off.

"I like it," she told her. "How much you care. I've always wondered why on earth someone like you would come here."

"But . . . I . . ." For once, words failed her friend.

Willa rose and walked over to the sink. She straightened out the crumpled washcloth in her hand and hung it up to dry. "I don't think I can go to Arthurdale," she told Miss Grace. "It's not right that I can and others can't."

"You don't understand," Miss Grace pressed. "As strange as it may sound, we need families like yours to go—families that are strong and loving and only need the smallest chance to thrive. Your going to Arthurdale will ensure that other towns are built for families like the Olivettis and the Settles. As you succeed, we all do."

Willa was not convinced. "I don't want help from those who don't want to give it." She stood in front of the window that overlooked the main street of the coal camp. The boarded windows and grimy wood looked bleak and desolate in the cold light of the electric lamps.

"Then go for me," her friend suggested. "Go where you can get the finest education we can give you. There will be a teacher there—an Ellen Clark—known as one of the best educators in the country. I've told her about you, how wonderful your mind is." She joined Willa at the window.

"I can't go," Willa insisted. Behind the company store, nearest the mouth of the mine, the houses of the black miners sat. The darkness over them was so impenetrable that Willa would never have known they were there— would never have given them a moment's thought, if it hadn't been for a woman who had helped her when all others had turned her away.

"Please, Willa." The words came out in a sob. Willa, shocked, turned to her friend. Hands clasped as though she were praying, Miss Grace had desperation in her eyes. Willa remembered the day Ves had told Daddy about Hawk's Nest; the men had been so desperate. Yet Daddy had insisted that men always had a choice. This time, the choice was Willa's to make.

"If I do go," Willa said, her voice fierce, "and I don't know yet if I will, but if I do, I'm only going long enough to learn how I can help. I want to make sure that those people sitting in the government don't forget about us. *All* of us."

Miss Grace nodded. "You look after Arthurdale for me, and I'll look after Riley for you."

With one last look at the street below, Willa turned from the window. "All right, then," she said. And when

Miss Grace opened her arms, Willa fell into them, grateful not to be alone.

Miss Grace's words were cold comfort the next day when Willa went down the hill to the Olivetti cabin. She had to knock twice before the lock was turned, and even when Roselia opened the door, her friend stood there unmoving, not welcoming Willa inside.

"I suppose you've come to say good-bye?" Roselia's cold voice was that of a stranger.

Willa *had* come to say good-bye, but the words never made it past her throat; not with Roselia standing there fuming and hurt. "I know why you're upset," Willa said. "I want you to know that I'm angry too."

Roselia folded her arms. "But you're still going."

"If only foreign-born families could go, what would you do?" Willa asked.

Roselia looked away.

"I talked to Miss Grace last night," Willa said. "And she's going to do everything she can. . . ."

"Do you know what my parents call me?" Roselia interrupted. "Do you know how they say my name? They call me Rose-a-LEE-ah." She sounded out the word carefully, the Italian sound of it rolling off her tongue. "Rose-a-LEE-ah. For hundreds of years, that's the correct way to say my name."

Willa stared at her.

"But you know what everyone in West Virginia calls me? Rose-ELL-ee-ah. Why? Because you folks can't be bothered to even try to say it correctly if you think it sounds too foreign."

"They're both pretty," Willa said weakly. She'd called her friend "Rose-ELL-ee-ah" herself. Everyone did.

Roselia unfolded her arms and pointed her finger so hard at her friend that Willa thought she was going to poke her, but instead Roselia turned it on herself. "I changed my name so I would be more American." She was furious, but that judging finger never wavered. "Me, who was born in this state the same as you. You can go to Arthurdale, Willa Lowell, but don't you ever forget that no matter where my family came from, I'm as American as you."

"I will!" Willa gasped out. "I mean, I won't! I promise I'll never forget."

There was no mistaking the earnestness in Willa's voice, and hearing it, Roselia relaxed a bit. Both were trying to keep from crying; Willa blinking back tears, Roselia's lower lip trembling. "Yes, well," she told Willa. Then she reached out and hugged her best friend as hard as she could.

But before Willa could respond in kind, Roselia was gone. She had closed the door between them.

Chapter Seventeen

The truck to take the Lowells to Arthurdale arrived just after daybreak. Many of the friends the family had made over the years had gathered about, wishing them well and calling out silly advice like "don't take any wooden nickels" as though a moment of silence would shatter the festive mood. Willa looked around, anxious to see if any of the faces were angry or resentful. There were none in the crowd; perhaps the ones who felt betrayed stayed away.

Willa knew this included Johnny and Roselia. Although Mrs. Olivetti gave all of the Lowell family (even Daddy and Ves) resounding kisses on both cheeks, even with Theresa and Seraphina promising to be friends forever, Roselia was nowhere to be found.

Though she didn't expect to see him, Willa couldn't help but look around for Johnny.

Just before noon, Daddy called everyone to the truck,

and they were on their way. Willa never even had the chance to say good-bye.

From the top of the hill, Willa caught a glimpse of her new home. In a bowl-shaped valley, white houses covered the fallow earth like clumps of Queen Anne's lace. Thick pine trees pointed to the pale blue sky. None of the homes were too close to its neighbor, but they were still near enough to be friendly.

"Wonder which one's ours," Ves said. He was leaning so far out of the back of the truck that Willa expected him to tumble out with every bump.

"I like that one," Willa said, pointing to a cottage in the shape of the letter *L*. Miss Grace had told her that some of the houses were called "alphabet" homes on account of their looking like *E*s or *L*s or *I*s from above. The streets, too, were named for letters; Willa couldn't help but think she'd feel at home in a place where you could make up words just by walking down the road.

"Who do you think lives there?" Ves asked, noting with a toss of his head the grand mansion stretching across the top of the tallest hill. The dark framed building had more windows than Willa could count and two rounded turrets like a castle.

"The operators, I guess," Willa answered. The truck started up again and she sat down with a thud as they lurched forward. She held on as they entered the village. "Likely even a government town has to have operators of some sort."

The truck pulled up in front of a tall white building with sloping wings on the left and right. Above the door was a large golden letter A. Daddy and the driver jumped out of the cab and went inside, but within moments they were back, Daddy dangling a set of keys and grinning like a kid.

Slowly, the truck wound its way along a gravel road, passing several houses. Some were the small and white "alphabet" cottages while others were two stories with cinder block bottoms and wooden tops. A few had been covered with a stone facade, which made them blend into their surroundings and not look so brand new. All were painted; all had windows that shone.

At last the truck stopped. "Here you folks are," the driver told them.

Willa stood up and stared. Surely there had been a mistake.

Daddy held the truck door open for Mama. Everyone else tumbled out, and the whole family looked at the house. Two stories high, it rose over them. The red bricks of the chimney made a friendly burst of color against the green pines.

Mama reached out and grabbed Daddy's hand, her

other arm clutching Rusty so tightly, the little boy cried out. "Waitman," Mama said in an awed voice. "My word, Wait, how on earth am I going to keep it all clean?"

Her husband leaned over and kissed her on the mouth, not in the least worried that the entire world could see. "I trust you'll find a way, Esther."

He handed her the keys.

Every day, Willa learned something about the house that made it easy to love. For the first time, she could imagine herself as a character in a novel, a person who lived in a place worth calling home.

To start, there was the furniture: chairs around the big kitchen table and beds so high Willa worried that she'd roll out while she slept and tumble to the floor. None of the pieces were fancy, but everything was well made and brand new. "They'll last us a lifetime if we take care of them," Daddy told them the day they moved in. One of Willa's new chores was dusting each piece at least once a week, but even the dust was clean and white, not the gritty, oily dirt that crept over everything back in Riley.

If Daddy loved the furniture, Mama gloated over the refrigerator. More than once Willa caught Mama opening the door for no reason at all and sticking her hand inside. "I just wanted to make sure it's working," Mama protested when Willa teased.

"Miss Grace had one, over in Fairmont."

Mama ran her hand down the door, lingering over the metal handle, though she didn't open it. "They say Mrs. Roosevelt insisted on buying them, though it's more than we need, if I'm honest about it. Still, it is such a luxury, having it here to keep food fresh."

"I'm just happy to have food to keep," Willa said.

But of all the luxuries in Arthurdale, none was more wonderful to Willa than the hot and cold running water. During the first early weeks that they were all settling in, Willa couldn't turn the shiny spigots without recalling every heavy bucket she had lugged up the hill.

Small as they were, even Kyle and tiny Rusty played with the house. Kyle soon figured out that his baby brother would giggle if he pushed the wall buttons to turn the electric lights on and off. The two of them would sneak off to an empty room and play to their hearts' content, or at least until Seraphina found them.

"Kyle's playing with the lights again," Seraphina would tattle. Willa bit her tongue; in Riley, she had often felt that she and Seraphina were growing closer—or at least they were on the same side—but here in Arthurdale, Seraphina seemed to be growing younger instead of maturing. Instead of running off to play in the creek (or whatever it was that Seraphina did), she stayed near her mother and the house. What hadn't changed was her younger sister's impulsive and sometimes aggressive nature: they hadn't been in the house a week before Sera had been jumping about and nearly toppled through the window of the bedroom the two girls shared. She'd stopped short of going through the glass, but the curtain she grabbed to break her fall came crashing down. Mama promised to fix it as soon as she had a moment, but every time Willa saw the crooked piece of fabric on its dangling rod, she felt angry and embarrassed. The government had paid for those curtains; the least Sera could do was show some care.

If that were only her biggest problem. Even Arthurdale couldn't banish the "ifs" in Willa's life.

"Hello sleepyhead," Mama greeted Willa one morning. "You're just in time for breakfast."

"Willa stole the covers all last night," Seraphina complained, picking up the pitcher of milk and sloshing some into her glass.

What a baby, Willa thought, as she joined the family at the table. "You should say, 'she stole them.'"

"That's what I said. You stole them."

"I did not," Willa said. "I was just correcting you, not agreeing." She poured hot brown sugar syrup over her stack of buckwheat cakes. When she put them in her mouth, the thin cakes seemed to melt before they had time to reach her stomach.

"You did," Sera insisted.

"Be still," Mama said, cutting Rusty's cake into tiny pieces. "There are plenty of blankets in this house for everyone."

"And we can always turn up the furnace," Seraphina reminded them.

Mama turned back to the stove and flipped the cakes that bubbled there. "Furnace or no furnace, we are not going to waste coal. There are more important things to spend our money on—feed for the cow, for instance."

"Can I have the Granny quilt?" Sera asked, and Willa wondered if this had been the whole point of her sister's whiny campaign.

"You know that goes on my and Daddy's bed," Mama said. Sera looked crushed, but Willa felt meanly glad. The quilt belonged on their parents' bed; the moment Mama had spread it out Willa felt for the first time that the Lowells belonged.

Daddy's boots stomped on the back stoop. He burst into the house, the cold rising like fog from his hat. "Any chance a man can get some breakfast before he heads off to work?" Kyle ran to greet his father, who picked him up and swung him about.

Moments like this, it was easy for Willa to believe in what Miss Grace had said; that it was better to have saved some than to have left them all behind. If only she could sit here among her own family every minute of the day, Willa wouldn't have such doubts.

Then came school. If anyone back in Riley had told Willa that going to school would make her so out of sorts, Willa would have laughed in her face. The hours she had spent with Miss Grace studying had been among the best in her entire life. Before the family left, Willa and her friend had considered the many subjects she would now be able to really learn: history, math, geography, and penmanship. There would be new books to read, and even newspapers delivered every day.

The new school had even more books than back at the Mission, but Willa never had a moment to browse, let alone read. Miss Clark, the teacher, favored what she called a "hands-on" form of learning; this meant touching and looking at and even tasting the world around them, but not reading much about it. Half of the time, they didn't stay in the classroom—despite the large maps on the walls and the plentiful supplies at every desk—and sure enough, when Willa stepped inside that morning just as the bell was ringing, the children all around her were still wearing their coats. Willa sighed—another field trip.

"We're heading up to the old Fairfax cabin," Miss Clark called out. Willa grimaced. They had already spent three days cleaning and working on the smelly old cabin, which reminded her of the shack back at the mines. Miss Clark told them they were going to restore the historical site, using materials found in and on the land. "It's all part of preserving your heritage," she told the students.

But Willa didn't want to preserve her heritage. She wanted to move upward and onward. What was the point of studying something from so long ago, when so much was happening right now? As the students left the schoolhouse and walked behind the large mansion that overlooked the town, Miss Clark rambled on: "The land where Arthurdale is built has a long and excellent history. This was once a plantation owned by Colonel John Fairfax, a friend of President George Washington. They fought in the Revolutionary War together, with John Fairfax serving as General Washington's aide. Washington was familiar with this land, having surveyed it for the great British landowner Lord Fairfax, when Washington was a young man." Miss Clark paused a moment and took a breath. "The surveying position was Washington's first real job, so you see, you don't have to start with something fancy to become a president of the United States."

Willa was bored. She wished she could read about it instead of having to march up this long hill. Up near the front, holding on to Miss Clark's hand, was Seraphina, listening as hard as she could. Willa slowed her steps until most of the group was far ahead of her; the ugly gray cabin was just ahead. While Seraphina and the other students followed Miss Clark inside, Willa turned and walked back home.

After that, Willa stayed away. She did her chores and read the few books Sera could bother to bring home; but the younger girl's forgetfulness often raised Willa's temper to the point of seething. Without the books, Willa took to writing down her own thoughts. She started with the idea of sending letters to Miss Grace, but as the work grew longer and longer, Willa found that this wasn't a letter at all, but a sort of story: facts and observations linked together by her own life.

When she was writing, Willa didn't think about missing school. She began dividing the papers into two piles: her public thoughts (mostly good: the house, the refrigerator) which became real letters, and her private musings (often bitter: Miss Clark, Seraphina) which she kept in a box beneath her bed.

Sometimes, though, ideas were too big to be simply black or white, like when she wrote about seeing the flag snapping in the wind by the Community Building. "I love seeing it, knowing all of the history that has gone into making this simple cloth mean so much to us," Willa wrote to Miss Grace in her neat, careful hand. "But I can't get Roselia, or Johnny, or Tori out of my mind. This flag stands for equality for all Americans, but

I know we are still a long way from that dream."

Paper to write upon, like the books, meant Willa continued to be dependent upon Seraphina, who was no better about remembering to bring enough of either home to suit Willa. Worse, Sera sometimes went into Willa's private box. More than once, Willa found some pages missing.

Sera, of course, denied it. "Why would I want your stupid old papers?"

"Because you can't believe the world doesn't revolve around you," Willa snarled. "You're such a baby."

By early December, bad feelings between the two had reached a boiling point; they were barely speaking. When Seraphina came home one day and prattled on about all they were learning in school (and had forgotten to bring home more paper and a book of poetry Willa had asked for), something in Willa snapped.

"We're learning about pioneers," Seraphina babbled to Mama at the sink. She sounded just like Miss Clark, Willa thought, stuck in the past as usual. "Pioneers didn't have things we have today. They lived in log cabins with bee gums for honey and made troughs for their mules and cows out of old logs." Seraphina turned on the spigot. "And they didn't have water inside their house, like we do."

"We didn't have water until we moved here," Willa taunted. "And we weren't pioneers, just poor."

"Willa!" Mama scolded.

"She can't do anything right," Willa protested. "And she steals my papers and things."

"I don't," Sera insisted.

"You do too."

"Girls!" The word cracked so sharply that they both looked up. "I've had just about enough." Mama glared at one daughter, then the other. "If you can't speak pleasantly, then don't speak at all." She turned back to the sink.

Seraphina's mouth dropped open. Willa was tempted to throw something into it. When the younger girl saw her sister's furious face, she burst into tears and ran from the room. Mama, her lips pressed so tightly together that her mouth made only the thinnest line, sent Willa out to feed the chickens. She said no more about it, but after supper she called Willa into the kitchen after everyone else had gone to bed.

"Sit down," she ordered her oldest daughter.

Willa did as she was told, but held her body rigid. She didn't want to be there, and Mama knew it.

"I know that the school hasn't worked out for you," Mama began.

"It doesn't matter," Willa mumbled. "I'm too old anyway."

"Willa," Mama said. She didn't look angry, but dismayed. "What's gotten into you?"

"It's awful, Mama." Willa couldn't stand seeing her

mother like this, but she was at a loss about how to make things better. "Why can't it be like it was at Riley? With Miss Grace?" Out of sheer frustration, she struck the table with her hand, enjoying the sting of it. "I hate it, going and cleaning that old cabin. That's not learning."

Mama didn't argue. "I admit, I don't understand everything myself. But look at the way Seraphina's doing. She's talking and learning and growing, Willa, and that's important too. Kyle's said more in the past few weeks than he's said his whole life. I used to worry about him, and now I think he'll be all right."

But Willa wasn't listening, slumped in her chair feeling sorry for herself. From the red dress in Fairmont to the school in Arthurdale, she didn't fit. Over in Riley, Johnny had thought her old enough to marry, but here she was no bigger than Seraphina to people like Miss Clark.

"I have to confess something to you," Mama told her. "It wasn't Seraphina who took your papers. It was me."

"You!" Willa could not have been more shocked. Or so she thought, until she heard the rest of it.

"I gave them to Miss Clark."

"What?"

Mama lowered her arms. "Look, I'll be the first to say I did wrongly. I'll be the first to apologize. But try and see this through my eyes: not a day goes by but you aren't scribbling away, and I can't help but notice that you grow more and more unhappy." Mama's face turned pink. "And you might not believe me, but I was trying to respect your privacy. You know Daddy and me aren't readers, and I didn't want to ask Ves or Seraphina. . . ."

Willa leaned back in her chair so hard it rocked. She ran her hands through her hair as though she might grab it and pull it out by the roots. Never in her wildest thoughts had she ever thought she couldn't trust Mama.

"You had no right . . . ," she began.

Mama reached out and took Willa's chin firmly in her hand. Willa tried to jerk away, but Mama held fast. "And you have no right to treat your family this way." She let Willa go, her body sagging. "I only gave Miss Clark the papers to send them to Miss Grace."

"Did she?" Willa asked, mollified a little; she trusted Miss Grace.

"I don't know," Mama said. "I don't think I explained things very well. She was too busy telling me just why she runs the school the way she does. Something about teaching children who have never learned to read—who have parents who can't read." A flicker of a smile passed over Mama's face. "That woman can run on when it suits her." She wrinkled her mouth just the way Miss Clark did right before she launched into a pitch-perfect imitation of a lecture about heritage.

Willa couldn't help but laugh.

"Anyway, we've been talking about what to do with you these past few weeks. Seems your Miss Grace gave her a glowing report, and she's eager to make the most of you."

With one finger, Willa traced the grain of wood on the tabletop.

"You're a very smart girl, Willa. Everyone knows that. And we all want to see you have your chance."

Some of Willa's anger began to fade.

"One thing we decided," Mama continued, "and Miss Clark agreed with me. You need to stay in school."

Willa's head snapped up. "But I don't want to go," she said.

Mama did not blink. "Your education is important, Willa. I trust that for all your book learning you will be smart enough not to throw it all away."

Willa sighed. More field trips. More lectures.

"Miss Clark would like you to take some of the younger children, and help them with their letters." This was something new. "You'd be a student aide, Miss Clark called it." Mama smiled at her. "Almost a teacher. And after regular school hours, Miss Clark would work with you one on one, just like Miss Grace was doing."

For the first time, Willa felt that Arthurdale had something to offer her—oh, it had already given her plenty, if you thought of her as one of the family, but until now, she hadn't been sure if she, Willa, should have come. There was so much to be done, after all, back in Riley, and few enough who could do it. Maybe she could become a teacher, and go back into the coal camps. No matter what, if she went to school, she would have access to books and paper again.

"One more thing," Mama said. Willa held her fingers still. "I don't know how this happened; if it was Miss Clark or Miss Grace's doing, but Mrs. Roosevelt sent you this."

Mama handed a newspaper to Willa.

When Willa read the newspaper, her eyes went wide. There, on the front page, was printed "A Letter From a Young Homesteader," followed by her own name. The next lines were her words, just the way Willa had written them: the story of the day the ice storm had gone through, creating slippery roads and trees that sparkled when the sun shone. Willa had described how lovely it was, and how much she could appreciate the beauty of it, because she knew her home was warm and dry. She reminded herself how this could never have happened in Riley Mines, where the trees were gone and the earth was bare. She wrote how the wind had screeched through the broken windows and blown the plywood doors open in the coal camp. "I worry about my friend Roselia, who couldn't come to Arthurdale because her mama and daddy were born in Italy. The government tells too many people 'no.' Washington, D.C., demands too much from the people they are supposed to serve. They turn away families like the Settles, even though their father has lived in this state as long as anyone. They judge and find wanting those like Granny Maylie, who cared for my mama when no company doctor would, only because of the color of her skin."

"This is my letter," she said. "Published in a real newspaper." Willa could hardly believe it.

Mama tried to look stern, but there was no mistaking her pride. "Miss Clark is very excited about your writings. She thinks you have the makings of a newspaper woman if you set your mind to it. If you go back to school, she'll try and help you all she can."

Willa looked down at the paper again; she couldn't seem to stop looking at it. The idea of writing for a newspaper was exciting. Working for a newspaper, she could describe the world around her, reminding people like Mrs. McCartney, in her snug house in Fairmont, that the world was full of families like the Lowells and Olivettis and Maylies; that each one deserved more than a passing thought.

I'll make them think, Willa decided; with words, I'll make my world so real that no one will be able to forget it.

Chapter Eighteen

Willa placed the last green fir decorations on the windowsill of the schoolhouse. Through the glass she could see the village of Arthurdale, white and frosty in a light dusting of snow. Miss Clark kept assuring all of the students that no bad weather was expected, but everyone kept double-checking just to make sure. "I think I see a patch of blue," Willa told Seraphina, who had come up behind her. "And there's another over the Community Building. You know what Mama says, if you have enough blue to make a pair of britches, the sun will shine."

Sera remained unconvinced. "I just want everything to be perfect."

"It will be," Willa said. "The school looks beautiful for the Christmas program tonight."

"I can't get over the lovely manger your father built for our Baby Jesus," Miss Clark said. "Truly fine work."

"Let's just hope the McAllister baby doesn't scream the whole time," Seraphina muttered.

Willa laughed. "First the weather, now the baby. You're just looking for something to go wrong."

"Well, I've never been in a play before," Seraphina said.

"None of us has," Willa pointed out.

The whole Lowell family was involved in the Christmas pageant—Daddy had built the sets and Willa was in charge of decorations. Mama had headed up the costume department; every night for the past two weeks the Lowell table was piled high with fabrics of every color waiting in turn to be made into angel outfits (including one for Seraphina) and shepherd head coverings.

The smallest children were to play the animals. Kyle's wooly sheep suit made him look like a little gray rain cloud. "Just like in *Winnie-the-Pooh*," Willa had told him (she had brought the new book home to read aloud together), which brought out his shy grin. He talked more now, but still mostly to Mama.

Only poor little Rusty, too old for the starring infant role and too young for everything else, had been left out.

And Ves. Ves hadn't taken any part at all.

Willa was so busy with her books and writing and helping around the house and school that there was no time now for walks with her older brother, even if they could have found a place as special to them as the old pio-

neer cabin had been. Ves wasn't interested in more education, and Willa could understand. As out of place as she
had felt, Ves, at nineteen, would have been even more so.

"What do you do all day?" Willa asked him one night,
when she was washing the dinner dishes.

Ves gave Willa one of his now famous shrugs. "I've
been helping Daddy, over at the woodshop. He's talked to
some men about taking me into the forge." Despite the
lighter workload, Ves always sounded tired; his tall, thin
body slouched against the doorframe.

Willa paused, hot soapy water dripping from her
hands. "You aren't happy here, are you?" she asked.

Ves sighed. "It's stupid, ain't it? We fought so hard and
so long just to make ends meet, and now that we got more
than enough, I'm not grateful."

Willa rinsed a plate and handed it to Ves. "The towel
is over there," she said with a nod.

"What?" He stared at the water dripping from the
plate to the floor.

"Might as well be useful around here," she told him.
"As I see it, you got far too much time on your hands."

Ves grinned. "Never thought I'd be happy to be doing
women's work," he said. He dried the plate and picked up
another.

"Things need to be done, whether you're a man or
woman," Willa told him. "And you did plenty of your

so-called 'women's work' over in Riley." Willa didn't want to admit that she actually enjoyed doing the dishes; not the work, exactly, but the pleasure of knowing that when the hot water cooled there was plenty more.

"I'm a miner, Willa," Ves said. He picked up a pile of dry dishes and put them into the cupboard. "I want to be in the mines."

Willa pulled the plug. "Are you serious?" she asked him. "No work, most of the time—and when you could get it, that was just another chance for you and Daddy to die down there." She shivered. Sometimes at night she dreamed that she was pulling down coal pillars, pulling the mountain down on top of her.

"But it's what I want to do," Ves answered. He smiled shyly. "I sometimes think the dust you breathe in makes you part of the mine itself. I feel like the mountain is part of me."

Willa busied herself scrubbing the already clean counter and sink, trying to understand. From the other room came Mama's silvery laughter and Daddy's booming voice.

"So what are you gonna do?" she asked, her voice low. She focused all her attention on a tiny piece of carrot that had stuck to the side of the sink; what she really wished was that she could scour these thoughts out of Ves's mind.

"I'm going back to the mines," Ves answered. "Maybe downstate, where the work's better." Willa realized that this was something he had thought about for a long time;

something that he had held inside of him because there was no one he could tell.

"Downstate," she repeated. Downstate was where Daddy had breathed in the white dust that had almost destroyed his lungs.

"They need organizers down there," Ves said, his voice eager now, young, as it hadn't been in many months. "I've heard that in some towns there are banners up claiming 'The president wants you to join the Union.'"

Willa felt a chill. She had hoped that moving to Arthurdale would get Ves off his labor union obsession. So many men had been beaten and killed trying to bring the union in that Willa actually feared the organizing more than she did the mines. A mining accident could be understood as an act of God, as man versus the mountain. Watching a guard beat a union man to a pulpy mess made Willa wonder what kind of world God had created.

"I'm leaving after the New Year," Ves told her. He seemed happier as he talked, and Willa remembered that first night on the mountain where just saying her fears out loud had meant so much to her. She forced herself to listen, although she wished she could plug her ears like Kyle did when the world became too much. "You know Daddy doesn't need my help around here. I'm not much of a hand at woodworking."

"Have you told them yet?" Willa asked.

Just then, the door swung open and Mama came in, her every movement swift and sure. "My, doesn't it look nice in here," she said. "I thought we'd make some popcorn." She bounced Rusty on her hip, his hair copper-penny bright.

"I'll do it," Ves offered.

"I'll help," Willa said.

Mama winked at both of them. "I was hoping that you would," she said. Willa and Ves watched the kitchen door close behind her.

"You haven't told them yet?" But she didn't need to hear Ves's answer to know. Mama wouldn't be so happy if she knew he was going away.

Willa awoke one cold December morning to hear Seraphina singing "Glory to God in the Highest." Burrowing beneath the covers (she had hoped with the play over, Seraphina would learn a new song), Willa had almost fallen asleep again before she remembered what today was.

Christmas!

Feeling a little foolish, Willa couldn't help but slip her hands beneath the pillows, wondering if maybe, just maybe, she would find a gift there, as the March girls had in *Little Women*. But her hand only found smooth, silky sheet beneath the fluffy pillow—all gifts in themselves,

Willa reminded herself, though she couldn't help feeling a little disappointed.

She wasn't the only one. Kyle, dressed in the long underwear he wore at night, poked his head around the door frame. "It's Christmas," he told his sister, his face grave.

"Yes, it is," she answered, equally serious.

"Will there be presents?" he asked. "Like the book?" Willa had read everyone *A Visit from Saint Nicholas* the night before.

Willa got out of bed and knelt in front of her little brother. The wooden floors were chilly through her flannel nightgown, but even so, she was plenty warm. When she hugged Kyle, he smelled like soap; he smelled clean and new.

"Let me get dressed, then we'll go see, all right?"

Kyle nodded. "I wait," he told her, and stood against the wall, just outside her room.

When they entered the kitchen, Mama greeted them from the stove. She was bent over the oven basting a chicken that had come from their own farmyard; the herbs floating like lily pads in the rich broth had come from the plants that lined the window over the sink. Willa breathed in rosemary (for remembrance? She'd been reading *Hamlet* with Miss Clark) and bay leaves; small sprigs of fresh parsley were tucked under the chicken's loose skin.

That's when she saw the presents.

Stacked like a pile of coal were five small round bundles, and if that wasn't enough, beneath them were boxes of all different shapes and sizes. Each was wrapped in brown butcher paper, tied with white string.

"When can we open them?" Seraphina asked. She'd already finished her bacon and eggs and pushed her plate aside. Her fork clattered when it hit the floor. "You said after breakfast."

"I meant after my breakfast," Daddy told her. He reached out and pushed the plate back to Seraphina. "And I think it would be nice of you to take the plate and put it in the sink."

Seraphina hesitated, then picked up the plate and bent to retrieve the fork before putting both in the sink. She came back to the table and asked if anyone else was finished, her voice polite almost to primness.

"I'm done," Ves answered.

"I'm done," Kyle repeated. He wasn't, but everyone in the family knew he'd jump off a bridge if Ves did it first.

"May I take your plates?" Seraphina asked. Willa watched in amazement as her sister went back and forth from the table to the sink until all the dishes were clear. She never dropped a single one. "Now?"

"Now, indeed," Daddy laughed. He reached out and tousled Seraphina's hair. Then he stood up and walked over to the table. He handed each child, from Ves down to little Rusty, one of the small presents.

Willa untied the string and opened the gift. Each package had an orange and some candy. The candy was hard, and shaped into squiggles that looked like ribbons. Each piece was a different size or filled with different colors: reds and yellows and greens and whites swirled in the bag that was larger than her fist.

Rusty was enchanted with the orange. He hopped down from Mama's lap and rolled it across the floor.

"He thinks it's a ball," Seraphina said. Kyle got down and rolled his and when it bumped into Rusty's, the littlest one shrieked with glee.

"Now for your mother," Daddy said. He picked up a large box and handed it to her.

"It's so heavy," she said, reaching inside and taking out a dark red coat, the color of cranberries. When Mama held it up and tried it on, she looked so beautiful that Willa caught her breath; the black buttons down the front couldn't shine as much as Mama's eyes. "It will be nice to be warm both inside and out this winter," she told them, and Willa realized that Mama had never had a real coat before.

Other gifts were passed around and opened. Seraphina also received a coat, blue to bring color to her pale cheeks, and Mama had bought Daddy a new folding carving knife, which he opened and closed with a satisfying snap. Daddy had made the little boys' gifts—a set of painted blocks for Rusty and a wooden train set for Kyle. Daddy showed Kyle how to blow into the engine's smokestack like a whistle, and a low, mournful sound filled the room.

When there was only one box left, Ves and Willa glanced at each other, wondering if perhaps there hadn't been enough money for everyone. Willa told herself that she didn't mind, but she couldn't help but think that maybe Ves didn't deserve a present—he'd been so gloomy when he should be glad. Or perhaps Mama and Daddy had decided that with all the books and learning she was given, she needed nothing else. She looked down at the orange and candy and decided that if she was the one left out, she would be brave about it; she would be proud.

But instead of reaching for the box, Daddy opened the door to the back stoop and brought out a traveling trunk with a handle, small enough to carry but large enough to put almost everything anyone would need within. He handed it to his oldest son.

"How did you know?" Ves fingered the leather straps that buckled across the front.

"I was your age once too," Daddy said, his voice husky with emotion. Mama was smiling, but the gladness did not quite reach her eyes.

Ves swallowed hard. "Open your present, Willa," he

said. "I want to see what you got." But Willa knew he wasn't really interested in her gift; he was still staring at his own.

Daddy handed Willa the last box on the table. It was the size of Mama's box and Seraphina's box, and Willa was sure it was a coat too. Certainly she needed one, as hers was threadbare and too short. She wondered what color hers might be.

Instead, there was a dress: a store-bought dress of red and black plaid, with a darker red shawl collar and a shiny black belt that Mama said was patent leather. It was the most beautiful, most grown up, most wonderful dress that Willa had ever seen. But not until she laid it gently back inside its box did she notice there was more.

Beneath a piece of tissue paper was a book, but when Willa opened it, she noticed that the pages were blank.

"Miss Clark thought you might like a real book," Mama told her. "She called it a journal, just like a news-paper person might use to write down ideas." Willa didn't quite know what to say. She tried to imagine what the pages might someday look like, filled with her own words.

"Won't we be all decked out for the New Year's party at the Community Building," Mama said.

"A party?" Seraphina asked. Willa looked up; this was news to her.

"A dance party," Mama said. "I'm told that Mrs. Roosevelt is coming."

Willa flipped through the empty pages of her journal. That will be the first thing I write about, she decided. A party with Mrs. Roosevelt!

Chapter Nineteen

Inside the community hall, the whole world was dancing. Everyone in Arthurdale—from the students Willa knew from school to the neighbors she had greeted, but had not been granted time to meet properly—floated over the smooth wooden floor as lightly as leaves bobbing in the current of a swollen river. Miss Clark was there, standing over by the doorway, and there, in the midst of it all, was Mrs. Roosevelt in a dark silk dress looking every inch the first lady that she was. As she flashed by, moving like a wave from one partner to the next, Willa studied her; she wanted to capture everything just so when she wrote it down in her journal.

Before she'd taken more than a dozen steps, someone swooped down and caught her up in a great hug. "Let me look at you!" Miss Grace exclaimed, taking Willa's shoulders in her hands. "You are as pretty as a redbird in that dress, Willa."

Willa didn't know when she had last been so happy. "I didn't know you were coming," she said, her joy rising like a trumpet.

"I didn't know if I could, not until the very last minute, so I asked Miss Clark not to tell." Miss Grace put her hands together and brought them to her mouth, but Willa could see the pleased expression beneath. "I can't get over how much you've grown—you look beautiful, Willa, if you don't mind my saying so."

"I don't mind at all," Willa said with a laugh.

There was a beat of silence and then the men playing banjos and guitars burst into a new tune. Mama and Daddy looked at each other. "That's 'Sally Ann,'" they both said at the same time. In the blink of an eye Mama had handed Rusty over to Willa and she and Daddy joined the dancers. Willa watched Mama twirl around and around, looking no older than Seraphina. Daddy's feet moved so quickly that Willa could hardly see them; the bass made a deep hum that reverberated every note through the soles of Willa's boots. (How glad she was to have bought the ones with the little heels last summer!)

When the set finished, Daddy was breathing hard and coughing a little, but down to his glistening skin, he shone as he looked at his wife. Mama's silvery hair was a little loose over her ears; she held onto Daddy's arm, keeping him close.

"I'm getting too old for this," Daddy groaned.

Mama hugged him to her. "Don't talk rubbish. You know it was on account of your dancing that I first made eyes at you," she said.

"Listen to her," Daddy told the family and anyone who might be listening. "Talking about making eyes at me. This woman has no shame whatsoever." When a new song swelled forth, Daddy gave Mama a little push towards Ves. "Take your mama out there and show her how the young folks dance," he told his son.

Ves grinned up at him and saluted. "Yes, sir," he answered. He turned to Mama and bowed; Mama made a neat curtsy and took his arm. They joined the others, taking part in the brilliantly colored sphere of movement.

Miss Grace put her hand on Willa's arm. "Let's go have some punch. I have so much to tell you."

Daddy reached for Rusty. "You go and have a good time," he said. "You can catch up with us later." Willa followed Miss Grace around the edges of the crowded room to the refreshment table.

"This is a marvelous party," Miss Grace said, handing Willa a glass. The fruit punch was so good that Willa held it on her tongue a moment before letting the cold smooth drink glide down her throat. "Sometimes I can't believe that Arthurdale actually happened." Mrs. Roosevelt passed by again, her face flushed with pleasure, brightening her homely face. When she saw Willa, she grinned so broadly Willa could count every tooth. Willa waved back, pleased that Mrs. Roosevelt had remembered her.

"I wish everyone in Washington could see this," Miss Grace continued. "Sometimes I wish that Mrs. Roosevelt could just pick all of you up and take you right there in front of the Capitol so everyone could see for themselves what we can do if we just give people a chance." She finished her punch and turned to her friend. "Your letter in the *Washington Post* was wonderful, Willa. Many government people read it."

Willa squirmed a little; as eager as she was to write for the newspapers, she could confess something to Miss Grace that had bothered her since she'd seen the clip. "If I'd known it was to be published, I would have put more work into it, made it a little fancier. I didn't write it for the government people, just for myself."

Miss Grace put her arm around her. "Let me tell you something, Willa. That work had freshness to it that all the journalists in Washington would give their . . ." She paused. "Well, they'd give their eyeteeth for it." Willa laughed, remembering the joke they had shared during those early days of the Mission. "I heard one of the most cynical congressmen in Washington say that your letter was the real thing. He knew you hadn't written it to change his mind, and that was the reason that it did. I hope you never lose that ability to see the world for what it is: the good, the bad, the ugly, and the utter wonder of it all."

"I still wish I'd known," Willa said, trusting that her old friend would know she wasn't complaining, just talking out loud as they had always done together. "Miss Clark is always going on about preserving our heritage, but I want to write what I see around me. Won't what is happening now be our heritage someday?"

"Absolutely. You keep on writing, and see if you don't make things change in the future, if not always right this moment. How has Arthurdale been treating you? I take it from Miss Clark that you haven't found it to be your Eldorado."

Willa paused. "No, I can't say that." She took another sip of punch. "But it is a place where I can get ready for the next part of my search for it." Pictures of Roselia and Johnny, Granny Maylie and Tori, too, flittered through her mind. It could never be Eldorado when so many were still waiting.

A man Willa had never seen before came up and asked Miss Grace to dance. Willa watched as her friend appeared to be delighted. She called the man by his first name, Bruce, and it was obvious they knew each other well. "Do you mind, Willa?" Miss Grace asked her. "It will only be a moment." The man wiggled his unruly eyebrows at Willa. He was dressed in a dark and official-looking suit, but if she looked closely, Willa could see how the pants were shinier with wear than the jacket. The Depression has hurt so many people, Willa reminded herself. All over West Virginia; throughout the whole United States.

She wondered what Mrs. McCartney would think of him.

"Go," she told Miss Grace, and watched as the couple moved from the edge of the room into the swirling center.

For a moment, Willa stood there all alone, watching everyone in the room. She could see Daddy, standing with Mama by the fiddle players. He held Mama's hand and he kept tapping his toe in his worn boots. Beside them, Seraphina and Kyle were spinning around until they were too dizzy to stand straight. They fell to the floor laughing and then picked themselves up to begin again.

Willa was surprised when she saw Ves on the floor with a girl named Rachael—someone Willa knew from school. She was laughing at something that Ves was saying, her long red hair flowing out behind her when she bent her face to say something in his ear. Ves nodded and when he passed by his sister, not three feet away, he never even saw her.

I'm going to miss Ves something awful, Willa thought. His new travel case was packed and ready to leave on the train downstate the next morning. Over the past year they had been through so much, and Willa felt that she was only now getting to know him, not only as her brother but also as the young man he was, with great hopes and dreams and more than his share of the Lowell stubbornness. Willa couldn't help but take some pleasure knowing that he was going to do the work he'd so longed to do, even if it involved real risks.

"Willa?" She raised her head. At first she didn't recognize the serious-looking man standing there, though there was something familiar about him. He wore a worn suit not unlike the one Miss Grace's dance partner had on, but he didn't look like a government worker. Not until he grinned did she realize it was Johnny.

"Are you surprised?" he asked, his voice cocky; he rocked on the balls of his feet as though he owned the whole world.

"Am I ever," she told him. "What are you doing here?" Just a month ago, hardly more than a few weeks, she would have rushed to him and hugged him, let him kiss her. But so much had passed between them that seeing him here, dressed in his shabby best, was like meeting him all over again.

He put his hands in his pockets, as if he, too, wasn't sure what to do with them. "I was afraid Ves would go and let the cat out the bag—that fellow never could keep a secret."

"Well, he kept this one," Willa told him. "Are . . . are you here to stay?"

Johnny glanced away a moment and shook his head. "Not me. I'm heading downstate with your brother for a while to join in the organizing fun. We're leaving on the same train, and he suggested that I meet him here before we go. Thought I might want to see you." He tipped his head and his eyes were as gentle as they had been during those hot summer days in the fields. "He was right—I'd hate to think I'd gone without seeing you in that pretty dress."

Willa blushed. "My hair's longer too," she blurted, feeling like an idiot the moment the words were out of her mouth.

He reached out his hand and stroked her head, pulling back almost the moment his fingers met her skin, but she could still feel the pressure there, as though he'd left a mark. "Your hair was always nice."

"That's what you always said," Willa replied, trying to take a deep breath in hopes of keeping her heart from beating right out of her chest. She could feel it there, pounding stronger even than the drum of the music. All that summer and into fall, she had been the one who always did the talking; now every word she'd ever known had flown right out of her head.

"You want to sit down?" he asked her.

"All right." They found two seats in the far corner, still in sight of the dancers but catty-corner from where the musicians stood. "The music here isn't quite so loud," she said.

Johnny leaned forward, speaking directly into her ear. "'Music I heard with you was more than music,'" he quoted.

Willa felt her entire body go warm, right to the tips of her fingers and toes. She could feel her stomach flutter. Her body had not forgotten how to be around him, even if her tongue had. "That's Conrad Aiken's poem," she whispered.

"I confess I cheated a little," he told her, a sheepish expression on his face. "I wanted something romantic to give you for our first Christmas together—and I think it's true enough, even if I didn't write it first."

"It's lovely," Willa managed to say. "Thank you."

"Roselia helped me find it, when I told her I was coming to see you."

"How is she?" Willa asked, suddenly nervous. What she really wanted to know was if her friend had forgiven her.

"She read that letter you wrote in the newspaper. Miss Grace had a copy and showed the whole town. They're real proud of you, Willa. I about burst my buttons thinking you'd once thought a lot of me."

"I still think a lot of you," Willa told him softly. The music had stopped a moment and Willa heard Mrs. Roosevelt's laugh rise like a birdcall in the sudden stillness.

"Roselia about swooned when she saw her name," Johnny said. "And she told me to give you a message. She wants to know why you haven't written her once since you went away."

Tears welled up in Willa's eyes. "I will write her," she promised. "Tomorrow, first thing."

Across the room the banjo began playing "Golden Slippers." Johnny stared out over the floor as it began to move again. "I don't know how long I'll be downstate," he said. "Ves is thinking a year, maybe two at the most. A lot can happen in that time."

Willa agreed. "I'm starting on the newspaper here in Preston County this spring. Nothing fancy yet, mostly fill-in work and writing bits and pieces where they need them. There's a whole new language that I have to learn—words like "leading" and "typesetting"—and I need to study grammar till I get every word right. Miss Clark thinks that if I work hard for them, after a while she might be able to get me into a journalism school, or maybe on at one of the papers in Washington, D.C."

"What would you do there?" He sounded as though he really cared; that he believed she could do it, and that gave her strength.

"I'm going to write for them—like that letter, only more. Right now, everything's just in my journal, about things here in Arthurdale, but I want to do two things. I want to take our world and tell people on the outside about it—remind people that ideas like Arthurdale are important, but we can do so much more."

"You'd be good at that," Johnny said.

"And I want to travel and see things—that way I can write about them and bring them back to people like Mama and my daddy, who might never have the chance themselves."

He still didn't touch her. "If anyone can do it, I know you can."

They listened to the music.

"Will you wait for me, Willa?"

Once again, Johnny'd given her a question she could not answer. Two years was a long time. Anything might happen.

"I don't want to be with anyone else," she said at last. "That's all I can promise you."

He nodded, as though he felt the same. "So what do we do now?"

"Well," Willa said, "I'd like a dance, but no one has asked me yet."

Johnny rose and stretched out his arms. "May I, my lady?"

Willa put her hands in his.

Author's Note

Arthurdale, West Virginia, is a real place, the first of many New Deal homesteads. My father was born there during World War II. I've made some small changes (for instance, government moves much slower in real life than it does in my novel), but I've tried to remain true to history. In the town today, you will still find the community center with the big letter *A* and Willa's "alphabet" streets. There is a museum showing what the Lowell home might have been like in the 1930s. For more information, please visit www .ArthurdaleHeritage.org.

Riley Mines is fictional, drawn from many coal company towns, but the poverty was very real. Eleanor Roosevelt did indeed come into these towns and offer hope, as did many missionaries, including Mary Behner. More information about these mining towns and their history can be found by visiting www.the-shack.org and www.as.wvu.edu/~srsh/history.html.

Photographs of 1930s coal camps and Arthurdale can be found at the Library of Congress website, www.loc.gov. The West Virginia Division of Culture and History is a wealth of information on coal mining, West Virginia, African Americans, labor union organization, the Great Depression, the Hawk's Nest disaster. Please see their website at www.wvculture.org.